Some Things You Love With Your Insides, Your Guts

A Novella

Joshua Rodriguez

Thirty West Publishing House

Some Things You Love With Your Insides, Your Guts

Copyright © 2024 Joshua Rodriguez

All rights reserved.

ISBN-13: 979-8-9895422-2-2
Cover art by Elias Mateo
Jacket design by Josh Dale
Edited by Caterina Alvarez
Printed in the U.S.A.

For more titles and inquiries, please visit:
www.thirtywestph.com

This one's dedicated to my grandma, Esther.

Rest in power.

Some Things You Love
With Your Insides,
Your Guts

OUT OF THE LOOP AT ALL TIMES (WE DON'T SPEAK; WE JUST GUESS WORDS)

Dogs bark in a cacophony, and it ripples across the neighborhood. It suffuses in a chain reaction—an implacable conflagration like a wildfire. Unremitting—refusing to subside. It gets to be that they aren't barking at anything in particular. They're just barking because other dogs are barking at other dogs barking at other dogs barking. It's like the big bang—suddenly a whole universe of something manifests—something wrung out of nothing like the Immaculate Conception—oblivion's bastard love child.

The Alleged Virgin Mary stares at a pregnancy test in her family trailer's bathroom—a calamitous cauldron—hands shaking—nails sand-tawny from chain smoking cigarettes—unblinking and trying to figure out how she's gonna break (and explain) it to her folks—how she's gonna explain to Big Joe she hasn't stepped out—eyes beady—pruned by terror—frangible voice lilting, bemoaning her perennial misfortune, 'Just my fuckin' luck—*of course* I don't even have to fuck to get pregnant,' guts dropped all over the damn floor—always missing out on the fun parts like unknowingly being served alcohol-free beer when you don't even like the taste of beer to begin with.

Out of the loop at all times.

No one makes it out uncorrupted.

Denial begets truth and truth begets denial. Belief is suspended over fire like it was making revolutions on a rotisserie—hanging like heaven caught on fire. A cavalcade of time—fusillade—luminous and vivid like Christmas lights festooning eaves and gutters—gliding by like highway traffic. Moments leading into moments leading into moments leading into moments. Ornamenting life like faded, haphazard prison tattoos. Moments swallowing moments swallowing moments swallowing moments—death nestled atop that food chain.

We don't speak. We just guess words that fall like slanting rain.

Sun-drugged and lethargic. I look in a mirror and am surprised to see something human-shaped staring back. Fumes fill my lungs and I cease to exist. I simply *am*, and life becomes a reverie as I teeter-totter over death. A symphony of dogs barking at dogs barking at dogs barking at dogs barking. The noise rises like tendrils of smoke, vanishing into the vast, flat, annihilating, smog-blighted sky.

Time is a flat circle. So is the world.

it's all downhill from here (a flat earth story)

SOME THINGS YOU LOVE WITH YOUR INSIDES, YOUR GUTS

Flat Earthers (FEs) are moving to Illinois on account of the flat topography. Like a mass migration to Mecca. A pilgrimage. After crossing state lines, the more sentimental ones stand at the edge of the highway, staring across the nondescript, level terrain, some even shedding a tear, wiping it away with one hand while the other raises a Kool cigarette to their lips, mumbling I can't believe it to no one in particular, not even themselves. Like they witnessed a miracle. Mauve dawn hangs overhead like a lampshade over the sun—translucent—a filter warping and discoloring light. Carter sits in the passenger seat and stares ahead despondently. The radio blares static; his father claims it helps attune to flatness. Like a hymn or stained glass rendering. They've been driving for hours.

His dad has custody due to his mom's drug habit. If only it wasn't so thoroughly documented, then Carter wouldn't be on this cross-country excursion to see nothing at all. The judge sighed when relegating custody: 'This brings me no pleasure at all—especially in light of recent revelations that he is, in fact, an FE,' disdain imbued these words and she couldn't even look his father's direction, 'but I have no choice considering the circumstances. I'm granting Mr. Craig custody of Carter.' Mrs. Craig didn't mind. She was too preoccupied with getting loaded again.

Her excitement could only be described as rapturous. She practically skipped out the courtroom humming a tune because she'd be done dealing with the deadweight of a child like a begrudged pallbearer.

Afterward, the judge—having witnessed the full gamut of a crooked system—resolved to enact change. She wrote and proposed a bill to render Flat Earth conviction analogous with neglect, like how courts perceive substance abuse. Ostensibly to revoke her own ruling. She's even advocated for having the severity of heroin addiction (among others) reevaluated in a litigious context. This precipitated Carter's dad's relocation to Illinois. To escape persecution. Friends and family abandoned him after being water-boarded with Social Media sermons; people he condescended to threatened his life; he lost his job because he kept harassing customers. He's sitting on a powder keg of paranoia, and Carter feels it.

Carter doesn't know where they're going. He just knows they sold everything they could and abandoned the rest. His dad doesn't even know where they're going. Wherever he's right—wherever truth's routed. 'Things are gonna be different,' his dad discloses in perfunctory reassurance. 'We're going where people know a thing or two' '....' 'I heard they only serve flat soda and flat beer, and you're only allowed to eat one pancake at a time in restaurants. Can you believe it? Sounds like paradise.' Even when all our Gods have abandoned us, we'll still genuflect before idols—we'll manufacture them. Because some things you love with your insides, your guts.' 'I gotta pee,' Carter says. 'Why didn't you go when we stopped?' 'I didn't have to then.' 'Goddammit, fine. One second. One second…'

TABULA RASA

Tabula Rasa is spray painted over *Lakewater*, the name official, like that constitutes legal amendment. It's the first thing seen driving in. They sleep in their car most nights and sometimes stay in dilapidated motels. But his dad's right. The soda and beer are always flat. However, Carter doubts it's some contrived idiosyncrasy—some cultivated quirk—like their iteration of a liturgical rite or tradition—Carter suspects it's more a failing these FE wackadoos sublimated into profundity. Like Catholics transmuting sufferings into gifts from God—Stockholm syndrome.

Churches welcome their congress with open arms. There's a podium and pinboard with photographs of flat terrain. Even the most overzealous geologists would be unimpressed. It's probably the first time this topography's been revered. Fluorescent lights flicker. FEs convene and talk in conspiratorial tones. Like Galileo's inbred, half-witted progeny. 'I think my phone's tapped,' Carter's dad says. 'I'm just glad I'm here. Where people can *think for themselves.*' They sometimes scheme but mostly commiserate.

Carter sits in back. His father says to listen—that Carter's old enough to understand. When meetings commence, Carter's dad acts like Carter dematerialized. There's palpable tension—words weighted with apprehension. It reminds Carter of when his mom brought him to stuffy NA meetings. Right down to the chairs, snacks, and coffee. Except at NA meetings, Carter actually learned a few things. It was a fly-on-the-wall vantage into his family's dissolution. Carter's mom was sober then. Which counts for something. He learned:

1. *His mom cheated.* 'But I didn't, like, *have an affair*,' her tone suggested that would be more dignified. 'I just needed to cop. I went to truck stops and solicited online. Withdrawing money only caused fights.' She stood and spoke in a way Carter can't help respecting since being trapped in what feels like a community college theater production of an insane asylum. 'Truthfully? I was eventually doing it outta spite. He wouldn't shut up about *the horizon.*'

2. *His favorite memories weren't what he thought.* 'I took Carter to Chuck-E-Cheeze one birthday,' she said. 'Just us two. I said I wanted to make it special. But I really just wanted to get loaded. I gave him cash to occupy himself and found a bar. I scored some shit, guzzled drinks, went back, and ate that cardboard pizza. Even fucked up I knew it was gross. I said I just wanted a special day with him. But using isn't exactly conducive to truth.'

3. *His father's FE affiliation was the nail in the coffin.* 'My husband—God bless him,' this was a year before losing custody—before the judge showed up unannounced to personally verify Carter's living conditions, 'he's obsessed with the Earth being flat—not believing *the lies we're taught.* Like Galileo was some fuck-up you keep around so you're not getting loaded alone. He's always chatting with strangers. He wants to move us to Illinois. He keeps calling it *Tubola Rosa* or some weird shit. What the hell's in *Illinois?*'

Carter absorbs it all.

APPLE TREES

Hal sits out front smoking cigarettes. The sun ripens and readies to set like a ship dropping anchor. He stares across the terrain—all 180- and 90-degree angles—squares, rectangles, and the occasional rhombus jutting out as shelter. Traffic encroaches like wildfire. It finally happened. They broke ground. They've lived here for generations. Hal remembers stepping off his porch into fields of apple trees. Now it's a different kind of field—cauterized—hard and vapid—charred like vulcanized smoker's lungs. Like what the Antichrist would be to Jesus H. He watched his dad wither down to nothing. His dad spent his entire life trying to be intractable and only substantiated the sole, immutable truth of existence: *we're born to be channels*. He remembers their last lucid conversation.

'*Closer*—come *closer*,' He motioned Hal nearer. The sour stench of death emanated. Death eats its way out; not its way in. 'Promise you'll take care of the house.' 'I will, Dad.' '*Promise*.' '*I promise*.' 'Even without me breaking your balls about it?' 'I'm sure you'll break my balls from the afterlife. I'll assume every morsel of bad luck is you getting even.' 'Always making jokes,' his dad waved dismissively. 'Tend to the house. *While you still can*. Before it's a parking lot.' 'Here we go...' 'You'll see.' '...' They assumed this was age—the garrulous incontinence of someone on their way out. 'Everyone's petrified of being paved over—of turning into a strip mall. It's the secret of our success.' '*Whose success?*' '*Our country's.*' 'Right, Dad...' 'Everyone's a cunt-hair away from having *off-ramp-front property.*'

Hal observes everything his dad evinced. His mom assured (and subsequently *reassured*) him his dad was just losing it. Or already lost it. There were mixed messages. Hal studies a flyer like an insurance policy. It crinkles and echoes across the phantom field of apple trees. The new road is uncorrupted—practically *billowy.* Like he could sink into and through it. Like the night sky—infinite—speckled with glistening pockets of interned sunlight. He never thought he'd turn into his father, but *c'est la mort.* Pretty soon they'll be routed. He remembers climbing apple trees and being chased out of the fields. Sometimes he hopes everyone's wrong—that there's some benevolent motivation behind paving over the world—that it's done for them, not to them.

He studies the terrain—ironed flat. He butts his cigarette on his heel. His mom hates the black skids on the railing and floorboards. He thinks about how the world must be flat because things would make more sense. How a flat earth would be like a consolation prize from God. How the imprecision of anything but 180- and 90-degree angles is a curse—an onus. He was outraged when they spray-painted *Tabula Rasa* over *Welcome to Lakewater.* Now he's coming around. He lights another cigarette, narrows his eyes: '*Flat Earth,* huh?' He reads aloud. Not to himself or anyone else. The sky goes purple-black like it was reflecting the asphalt. Or vise-versa.

BEHEMOTH

If Hal's learned one thing, it's expectations beget disappointment. Paradise is ruined by hanging around. Like the *Garden of Eden*: even if Adam and Eve didn't eat the apple (though most folks can't resist free doughnuts, let alone the fruit of knowledge), things wouldn't be any better. They'd have kids. Their kids would have kids. Each generation reproduces with itself—a recursive incestuous loop. It'd be nightmarish—populated by mutant tribes after generations of inbreeding. The *Garden of Eden* would end up being *The Hills Have Eyes*. Nothing's inviolable—nothing's sacred—once we've touched it. What could've been is only superior to what is because it's nonexistent. Hal's at a meeting in a church—churches are shoehorned in wherever they fit.

People talk about their weekends, families, prospective holidays—they whisper, touch shoulders in consolation. A kid sits in back. He looks about ten. He's distended—disproportionate from unremitting incursions of growth spurts. It feels like everyone's talking around the flat earth—the two-dimensional elephant in the room. 'You really have to go during fall,' someone says. 'The leaves are gorgeous, and you miss tourist season.' Hal helps himself to coffee and doughnuts. The pinboard has pictures of nondescript expanses of land.

'We need a new landscaper,' Hal hears. 'I told you our guy's the best.' 'I wanted to give these guys a chance, but they don't pay attention to details.' 'Look where we're at. You can't expect everyone to pay attention to details.' 'What's the world coming to?' It's unceremonious—like a social club. A man goes to the kid—presumably his father— whispers and pats his head—the boy nods—voices crescendo in a cacophony. Hal has a cigarette, finishes his coffee, and refills it. He doesn't know what he expected, but it wasn't this. The highway's interloping and there's nothing he can do about it. He doesn't know what this will do but at least it's something.

'Everyone—your attention *please*,' a man walks to the podium. It's desultory—like it's their first meeting. The kid's stoic. Hal's heard him and his father sleep in their car. His dad works odd jobs when he can. 'Let's get started,' the man at the podium says. 'First thing's first: *new member introductions.* You don't have to come up here. Just stand. Don't be shy—we don't bite.' Hal sits beside a behemoth of a man who smells the part. The man at the podium nods at Hal. Hal stands, talking awkwardly.

'My name's Hal. I saw this flyer...' Hal can't peel his eyes from the photographs—there's even a landscape portrait (presumably by someone in attendance that's even less interesting than its subject) hung like a toddler's finger-painting on a fridge. The land's flat, gray, and depressing. Like the missing link between nature and parking lots—an evolutionary rung toward measureless, metastasizing highways. Hal gets more coffee and doughnuts and watches from the nosebleeds. The kid leans over, whispering, '*Flat earth*—it's all downhill from here.'

A TRAIL OF HEADLIGHTS

Carter and his dad wait in line at the town's only drive-thru. This is the day's only refuge—the only time *Flat Earth* and whatever else governs his father's head isn't foisted on him—the only time he can ask questions without his temerity being resented—the only time his father asks *him* what *he wants*. It's sanctified somehow. The line's long and snakes around a building. Carter's stomach growls. They'll be waiting a while.

He thought of the man who called himself Hal. He stood the entire time before leaving with an inscrutable expression like he got in a pool with his phone in his pocket—steeped in that dispiriting aggravation for hours. He hasn't bought in yet. But Carter knows Hal's eyes will glaze over, too.

His dad looks in the rear-view mirror. Carter knows what he's thinking: *this is somehow evidence of a flat earth.* Carter could shit in the parking lot, and his father would designate the fact it didn't roll empirical evidence. 'It's cold,' Carter says. 'Are we sleeping in the car during winter, too?' 'Dunno.' 'We'll freeze to death.' 'We'll figure it out.' 'Why can't we get an apartment?' 'It's not that simple. We're refugees.' '...' 'Listen—*I've tried*, but so many FEs came for asylum. It's saturated.' 'We could move somewhere else.' 'What kinda talk is that?' He slaps Carter's head. 'Imagine what we'd forfeit if we went somewhere else.' '...' 'Look at those cars lined up—the trail of headlights. We can see flat across them. It might reduce me to *fuckin' tears.*'

They've waited 45 minutes. The only time Carter's seen lines comparable is when they visited his grandmother in Dinuba, a farming town in California. They visited national parks and waited hours for admission. At a drive-thru at least there's a payoff. Not just mountain ranges and bushes. 'Tumors treated like double ds,' his dad says. Carter's worried about the Illinois winter. His father doesn't want a permanent residence. They'll be easier to find. The judge's unannounced visits haunt him—her holding up FE literature like an admission of parental inadequacy. One parent can't keep a job to get an apartment; the other refuses. Whatever the opposite of the lottery is, Carter hit it big time. 'Things'll turn around.' '...' 'They're putting me on tour. People need to hear the truth about the Earth and our persecution.'

His dad's attained some derivative of celebrity—celebrity's degenerate, junky grandbabies. He repeatedly told their story until he became the paragon of their plight. 'We'll make good money telling our truth,' Carter's dad says. 'What about me?' 'You'll be fine. We're homeschooling you, anyway. I don't trust their agendas.' Carter waits for his day's first meal at 7 PM. '...they're talking about another mass pilgrimage...' Carter hates waiting but it beats sitting in the passenger seat and staring out the window in abandoned lots all night. Carter thinks about the national parks and how they couldn't hold a candle to this. 'They say

it's global warming,' Carter says. 'Don't get me started—
that's why I'm homeschooling you.'

GIANT SNAKE

Hal's wired. Not from overstimulation or irrepressible excitement, but the opposite. He noticed the kid observing him, still as a mannequin—not just when he spoke—when he stood in back trying to piece together that puzzling situation, too. The images pinned on the pinboard resembled the desolation that superseded the apple trees. Hal gets a beer, his weed, pipe and goes to the patio, has a cigarette, and scrolls through his phone, raising the can to his lips. He's nauseous from the doughnuts. But he'll go back. He still harbors that conviction: a flat earth's a consolation prize from a god whose whole fist is on the scale.

Hal takes a hit of pot. Looking out, he sees FE encampments. He sees fires and tents. They covered the gamut at that meeting, but he still couldn't recount the general conceit. Other than the earth is flat. But that's like saying a church service is about the grace of God. Hal watches a video claiming global warming is increasing the earth's temperature, allegedly enlarging snakes. Like during prehistoric times. It claims more creatures like this could emerge. The encampments snake across the horizon, writhing with dancing firelight. As far as he's concerned, discerning between global warming and natural progression is like discerning between radioactive mutations and evolution— 'like discerning between mob rule and democracy,' as his dad often said.

His phone rings. Who the hell's indecent enough to call at this ungodly hour? 'Hello?' 'Hey, it's Rick.' 'Shit. It's been a while.' 'Yeah, too long...' Hal wants to come out and ask what his brother wants from him. There's no other reason they correspond. 'I'm just checking in.' 'You drunk?' 'Kinda.' 'Me, too. It's the only time we get sentimental. How's St. Louis?' 'Oh, well, that arch is the only thing this place has going for it. That's actually why I called.' '...' 'I'm sick of living here—I wanna come home.' 'Oh...' 'I might move back this week if that's OK with you guys.' 'That's up to you. We'd love to have you.' *Shit—this is the last thing Hal needs.* 'Is tomorrow too soon?' 'Tomorrow's not soon enough.' 'I appreciate it. I really do.' 'You're family. What am I supposed to do?'

He'll be in town late the next evening. At least Hal has some time to get things ready—to prepare a bed and inform their mom. Whether it's for good or not (and for *whose* good) is unclear. Still, this feels serendipitous—like a sign. His brother put him onto Flat Earth. Hal wonders if he'll attend meetings with him. But Hal isn't getting his hopes up—his brother's still his brother. When Rick moved to St. Louis, the only way he could renew his driver's license was with a court summons for unpaid parking tickets. Hal watches more videos about snakes engineered by nature, God, or *whatever.* He looks at the encampment, unsure if it's a husk shucked off or a snake preparing to strike.

HOMECOMING

Garbage bags in the backseat are stuffed indiscriminately with dirty and clean clothes. Laundry's done sporadically—it's an expense and the last thing on his dad's mind. His dad tries explaining why he's so predisposed—so absent—he calls it state of consciousness. 'A flat earth means 2 dimensions. *Binary existence.* You're all in or all out' '...' Carter's homeschooling's on hiatus—his dad declared an extended summer vacation. Now it's winter and it's still summer vacation. Time's a flat circle. So is the world. Water bottles roll around the car filled with urine. They can't always pee where they park for the night, and waiting is impossible under such biological duress. Besides, even if they could pee publicly, the cold makes Carter's skin tauten and ache. And to shit? We'll leave that to the imagination.

Layers of trash are matted down like stratified sediment—like they could determine when what was consumed and discarded by its proximity to the surface. His mom's car was the same. There's probably a whole ecosystem of creatures here, too. Today's different. His dad's affixed importance to it. 'I'm dropping you off here,' his dad says at the Laundromat. 'I'll be back when you're done. It's time you pulled your weight anyway. Just do laundry and sit tight.' 'Where are you going?' 'A very important meeting.' The sun's out but it's nippy. Carter's jacket's thin—like a creature maladapted to their climate. He carries garbage bags of clothes. A man's passed out inside.

Carter's seen him at meetings. He doesn't look any more alive than he does now. He smells like his mom after a bender. Carter did his own laundry at home before his life was disassembled. He had no choice. He inserts coins. The machine clinks and clanks, digesting them. Like rancid food generating food poisoning. 'You see that guy?' Patrons talk quietly. 'Passed out?' 'Or nodding out.' 'That's what those FE Crazies are bringing. Kids can't even play outside. Remember playing all day in those fields without a worry? That's gone.' 'Those fields are gone, too.' 'You heard about Woodcreek?' 'Uh-uh.' 'They're building a compound.' '*Christ*—they really drank the Kool-Aid.'

They mean Carter too. He can't help getting offended. The unconscious man sits upright. Carter observes him with sympathy he resents the others for not affording him. Carter waits, hearing plenty about his father's people— '*the scourge of FEs.*' He has enough quarters for half their laundry. He knows how his dad operates and prioritized (what little) winter clothing (they have). His dad pulls up and honks. They look at the car, then at Carter. They didn't notice him—they're stunned—he was a mural on the wall. His dad's chipper, 'How'd it go?' 'I didn't have enough quarters.' 'Oh. Sorry.' 'I made sure to wash winter clothes first.' 'Homeschooling's learning you right after all, huh?' Carter's dad drives with newfangled intent. 'I have good news.' 'Where are we going?' Carter asks. 'Home, son. We're finally going home.'

CENTER OF THE WORLD

When Rick arrives, their mother's asleep. Hal's watching YouTube videos and smoking pot, which he's learned not to do around his mom—she has certain preconceptions. But Hal doesn't hold it against her. It's what she was taught—which is near the heart of his FE intrigue. Last they saw each other, Rick was lean, wiry, and working in waste disposal. Since then, his voice changed. Hal can't imagine what else has. He observes the FE encampment. He wonders what constitutes a compound. What criteria does a shantytown have to fulfill? He drinks beer but paces himself. Not out of propriety, but it'll be misapprehended as weakness. Holding your liquor's a virtue in their family.

The lights snake across the horizon—animated by dancing fires. Finally, there's a knock. Hal answers. They study each other through the screen door. Rick looks thinner—gaunt, his face full-grain leather. Hal can only imagine what he's thinking. Rick settles into his old room. He takes a shower and Hal brews coffee because that's what he's supposed to do. Finally, Rick emerges, hair matted down wet. 'How was the trip here?' 'Good. I left later to beat the traffic.' 'Yeah.' 'Sorry to keep you waiting.' 'No worries. Mom tried staying up.' '...' 'She wanted to, though.'

'You quit your job?' 'It was mutual. I hated working there and they said I wouldn't stop harassing people about, well, never mind.' 'About what?' 'Flat earth?' '...' 'I knew you wouldn't get it.' 'I actually went to a meeting.' 'No shit?' 'I was curious. And you, well, wouldn't stop harassing me about it.' 'I was a regular in St. Louis. It's a whole new world. What'd you think?' 'I'm not gonna lie—it wasn't what I expected.' 'Is that good or bad?' 'Jury's still out.' 'Once you start understanding and, like, accepting, things become clearer.' 'I just need something. It's like right before Dad passed. He always said the whole world was gonna be paved over.' 'He said a lot of crazy shit.' 'But was it crazy?' 'I don't know, Hal. I'm too tired for this.' 'Of course...' They go out and smoke a bowl. They're fixated on the encampment.

'They're FEs,' Hal says. 'More arrive each day. People talk like it's an epidemic—a plague.' 'That's how they talk everywhere. It's persecution.' 'They call themselves *refugees.*' 'Aren't they?' '...' 'Have you been to that compound?' 'No.' 'It feels like the epicenter of meaning— the true center of the world. Not some make-believe volcanic core.' '...' So, it comes full circle. Less like an explorer circling the globe and more like a patient in a psych-ward deliriously walking the circumference of their room—like a defective shopping cart stuck in a turn—like a delivery driver with an incorrect address—like being trapped in a washing machine. That kind of full circle. 'Let's go,' Hal acquiesces. 'I was worried you were a lost cause.' '...' 'Let's hit a meeting, too.' Hal doesn't know what he feels—it's indefinite and unformed.

NEW TENANTS

They arrive at the compound. Carter's dad conducts himself like an A-list celebrity entering a studio lot. He doesn't use turn signals. He told Carter, 'It's so they aren't a step ahead of me.' 'Who?' 'You know—*them*.' Carter dropped the topic. He recognizes dead ends when he sees one. A chain-link fence encircles a sprawl of tents and fires. This isn't what Carter expected when his dad said home. But, still, it's unsurprising. 'This is it,' he says to Carter. 'The Settlement.' His dad expects him to be blown away—to have his jaw on the ground like after he saw The Lord of the Rings for the first time. Carter surveys it disinterestedly.

Their car smells like laundry detergent competing with unpleasant smells for prominence—pervasion. Like what FE hysteria is to *Lakewater*. People don't look particularly sanguine—but they don't look unhappy either. It's something suspended between the two. Carter's dad honks at people and waves. 'They can't get us anymore. We're safe.' 'Are we sleeping in tents, too?' 'It'll be like camping.' 'But it's cold.' 'It's just temporary until construction's completed.' 'Why don't we come back when it's completed?' He smacks Carter's head, 'You need to learn the value of sacrifice.' '...' 'It'll be fun. We'll even have a heater.'

Carter watches the encampment wheel by. People cook over fires. Even people living out of tents eat better than him. Tents are patched. Faces are soot-blemished—hair's greasy and long. It looks like Nu-Metal Music Festival Grounds and smells the part. 'It's good for your health, too,' his dad says, 'Beds aren't good for your back. We should sleep on hard flat surfaces. Like the earth.' 'But it's uncomfortable.' 'What'd I say about sacrifice?' They turn into a vacant spot. 'I need to check-in. They forgot to lay out our gear, too.' '...' 'I'll be back soon. Just hang out and wait.' Carter's dad leaves. He obviously doesn't know where he's going the way he looks around to orient himself.

Kids approach. 'Hey,' one says, 'you just arrive?' 'Yeah.' 'So, you're the newbie.' 'For now—we'll probably leave soon.' 'No one leaves.' 'We have a car.' 'Everyone has a car at first.' 'What do you mean?' 'You have to give it to him.' 'To who?' 'You'll see.' 'What happens to it?' 'He sells it— they're always talking about money here.' '...' 'My dad says if I work hard, I can be treasurer one day.' '...' 'I'll be in charge of all the money.' 'We can leave without a car. It's a free country,' Carter parrots. 'You're only allowed to leave for work. Family has to stay. Any money earned goes to *The Cause*.' 'The Cause...?' 'That's why I wanna be treasurer— imagine all that money. My dad was an accountant, too. He says it's in our blood.' '...' 'Ask us if you need to know anything.' The kids leave. 'Carter—Carter!' his dad ambles toward him. 'You have to see this. You have to see *The Wheel*!'

AN INVITATION

Rick submits job applications and helps run errands. He even accompanies Hal to meetings and helps Hal orient himself to FE discourse. When it's Rick's turn to speak, his voice breaks: 'My brother finally came around. I'm proud. I've been to my share of meetings...' They eat it up—treat him like royalty. He drops names—talks about Rich in St. Louis—shows pictures of them together, arms draped over shoulders.

They're smiling so big (and unrestrained) it can only be described as unhinged—so intensely there it isn't there at all. Like inverted paranoia, how unrelenting suspicion and distrust eventually manifest what you feared most. Rick ingratiates quickly. Hal's still dislocated. Showing up baked isn't helping—it's always had the opposite effect. They attend three consecutive meetings before relocation:

1. ***Rick introduces himself.*** Everyone fawns over his story and fabled St. Louis connections—the real frontline of this sanctified territory. Hal tries (unsuccessfully) to deduce the brand of the cookies by taste. Rick tells a story about someone he knew who didn't want to enlist but jerked around recruiters. He wanted to see a doc. He was into regular maintenance. He calls him an exemplary FE.

2. ***Rick shares St. Louis discoveries.*** Hal stares at the pinned pictures. He wonders if we've evolved to need asphalt like how turtles need shells and are all soft, vulnerable tissue beneath. Maybe that's why we need a Flat Earth too. Rick retells the story. Without insurance, it was the only way for his friend to get a physical.

3. ***Rick listens quietly.*** Rick says, 'I want to listen. I've talked too much.' 'So wise...' Hal drinks coffee, listens to Rick's story. His friend couldn't stand the government (cue a hearty applause) but was neurotic about his health. He traveled town-to-town feigning interest in enlistment, alternating between branches.

'That food always fucks up my stomach,' Hal says in the car. 'I can't resist it, though.' '...' 'So, what'd that guy want to talk about?' 'What guy?' '*C'mon.*' Rick smiles inscrutably, 'An opportunity.' '...' 'We got it, Hal,' Rick speaks like shaken up soda—carbonated and pressurized—effervescent like they haven't had in years. 'Got what?' 'An invitation to *The Settlement.*' 'I don't know...' 'It's a once-in-a-lifetime opportunity. Even if you're unconvinced, do it for me. It's like we talked about: half of FE conviction is sacrifice.' 'When do you wanna go?' Hal sighs.

They drive to *The Settlement* the next day. 'We gotta see *The Wheel*,' Rick beams. Familiar faces abound. Everyone's unwashed. They don't look happy or unhappy. Hal observed Rick go from group to group, retelling his story. It was like monitoring brain activity seeing different clusters engage, activate, and deactivate. 'That story you've been telling...' Hal begins, turning down ramshackle roads as Rick reads directions scrawled on cardboard—arrows for *HQ*, *The Wheel*, *Bathrooms*, etc. 'You made it up, right?' Rick smiles, 'Only way to get invited.' People crowd around the giant wheel. The air's electric—fricative. 'It's real now, though, ain't it?' Rick slaps his back as they enter the fray.

CUL-DE-SAC

People weep at The Wheel. Some genuflect (Hal calls it histrionics). Others circumambulate it. Carter's dad speaks like he's witnessing a miracle. 'Can you believe we're seeing it?' Hal maneuvers through bodies like an obstacle course. Hal's worried they'll lose each other, and he'll be stuck waiting. Hal just wants to go home, get stoned, sit on the front patio nursing a beer, chain smoke cigarettes and stare at the asphalt expanse, wondering if it's the cadaver of those images on the pin board—a carcass to pick at. Rick moves effortlessly like the crowd was porous for him but impermeable for Hal. It smells worse the deeper he gets.

'Let's get closer,' Carter's dad says. 'I don't like crowds' '...' 'I can wait. I might go back anyway.' 'You know the way?' Carter nods. 'Ask for help if you need it. People here are family.' *That's not a high bar*, Carter thinks. Carter stares at the wheel. Part of him wants to go back—maybe see what those kids are up to. But he can't peel himself away. Not because of some magnetism, but because he feels like something will happen. Hal goes in circles, 'Excuse me, ma'am. Have you seen my brother? He's about so tall with long hair and a goatee. He's rail thin and pale. No? Shit, all right. You're right, ma'am. That does describe most people here.' And so on.

Carter's dad wouldn't shut up about *The Mission*. 'We live in an egg—we're just waiting to hatch—actualize. You're either unborn or born. It's a Flat Earth—a binary existence. This wheel would topple if the earth were round. But it's stable.' 'They dug a trench.' 'You think a trench could restrain it from falling when the world's supposedly spinning like that?' '...' 'Wait until you hear about the moon.' 'The moon?' 'It's a hologram.' Hal keeps looking. It's familiar—like the world. Impossible to disentangle—roads and highways inextricably intertwined. You take one turn, then another, then another. Time's a flat circle. So is the world. But every road eventually leads to a cul-de-sac—a dead end. And, at dead ends, with nowhere to turn, you end up turning on others.

Hal escapes the crowd—pushing against the current. He catches his breath, has a cigarette, 'This Flat Earth shit's gonna make me flat line.' Rick comes running with a goofy grin, 'Where'd you go?' 'I was looking for you.' 'I have good news. I found the guy I talked to yesterday.' 'So?' 'We can start.' 'Start what?' '*The Dig.*' 'That was serious? This feels like jumping the shark.' 'You still believe in sharks?' 'Can we leave already?' 'Let's sleep here.' 'I wanna sleep in a bed.' 'Sacrifice...' '...' '*The Dig*'s starting early. It'll be easier this way.' 'You stay then. I'll go home.' 'Not possible.' 'Why?' 'Two-dimensions—we need to come in twos. If I'm alone, I can't stay.' It's like they hijacked Noah's Ark. 'C'mon— *please.*' 'Fine—but we're leaving tomorrow.'

DIG, DIG, DIG

Carter's dad snapped in Dinuba, after visiting the National Parks Carter's dad denigrates as subterfuge—a government-funded art installation. (Carter's vocabulary is derived from his dad's ranting—though he often discovers his dad uses words incorrectly.) After that trip, everything changed. It was like passing out drunk before a meteor hit, pulling yourself out of a stupor, and piecing together what's different (apart from the carnage, debris, and altered climate). But people snap all the time. The moment he snapped wasn't when his grandmother needed legal representation because she flooded a neighbor's car. To this day, if the topic arises, Carter's dad says, 'The hose was attached to her house,' in rehearsed astonishment.

Hal worries they'll sleep in the car—everyone here looks accustomed to sleeping on anything but real beds. They're given a generator, radiator, cooler, beer, and blow-up mattresses. Others eye them with envy. Rick won't shut up—they chain smoke in the tent, occasionally opening the flap. Hal wonders what Rick did to earn preferential treatment—it isn't something they've been relegated. It often felt carcinogenic—avoided like smoking cigarettes. 'This is what purpose feels like,' Rick says. 'Do you feel it?' 'I feel something,' Hal says as weed-induced paranoia apprehends him and rubs his face in his every regret like an abusive owner potty-training a pup.

The moment Carter's dad snapped like a toothpick was when his grandma used a toothpick. It wasn't during their wedding ceremony when she audibly criticized Carter's mom—from her pedigree to her truck. She always complained about her pot-smoking neighbors. She called Carter's dad, incensed, 'I'm calling the police, *mijo*. I'm not living around druggers.' Before running errands, she covertly covered a toothpick in glue and jammed it in the lock. Carter's dad beseeched her for reasons. 'I don't want them breaking in.' 'Who?' 'My neighbors.' (They were the same age and retired.) 'You know what people do to get their fix.' She couldn't help bashing his mom. 'They asked for clippings from cut flowers.' 'So?' 'They'll probably sell them in Mexico. I threw them away.' Carter's dad spent hours calling locksmiths. Time's a flat circle. So is the world.

Rick wakes up first and gets them coffee made over a fire. Hal overhears conversations. Everyone talks in flat circles about Flat Earth—ignorant in their curiosity— creative in the most uncreative ways—so open-minded it's prohibitive. They smoke a bowl and cigarettes. 'Ready?' Rick asks. 'Yeah.' 'There's one thing...' 'What?' 'They have to blindfold us.' 'Fuck that.' 'Have faith.' 'Easier said than done.' Rick and Hal walk to a loading site—blindfolded ranks stand at attention. They join them and ride in the bed of a pickup. When they arrive, Hal doesn't know where he is. It's flat—all terrain looks identical. It feels like summer. They sweat. Hal's whole body aches. They dig like they're digging for oil. 'What are we digging for?' Hal asks Rick during a water break—speaking while digging's impermissible. 'You'll know in time.'

SHOVELFUL

Hal throws dirt over his shoulder—stabs his shovel into the ground—throws dirt over his shoulder—stabs his shovel into the ground. Time's a flat circle. So is the world. His muscles ache. Sweat drenches his face. It's like scooping unthawed ice cream. Hal works mechanically, like he's automated—like a piston in a combustion engine (which isn't exactly unwelcome speculation around the encampment—he heard plenty of that talk the night before). It's like digging for buried treasure. He doesn't know what they're digging for. An irascible, diminutive man (the two are likely related) bellows, 'Urgency, people. Faster!'

Carter's dad is back and forth all day. Sometimes he comes back with provisions—putatively if meetings go well—and he speaks with effusive hope—one so far gone on the spectrum it's approaching the opposite end. 'We have a new heater,' he says. 'That's just the beginning. Soon we'll get started.' 'With what?' '*The Tour*. The rest of our lives.' 'What about school?' 'Real knowledge—real truth—isn't taught.' '...' 'We're gonna be filthy, fucking rich.' 'What's *The Dig*?' 'It's a special mission.' 'Do I have to dig?' 'You'll have the privilege of digging. You have to learn the value of sacrifice.' 'You don't dig.' 'Start packing. Say goodbye to your friends, too.' 'What friends?' 'You crack me up.'

After *The Dig*, Hal feels like a butted cigarette. Rick was inexhaustible—he stabbed his shovel into the ground—threw dirt over his shoulder—stabbed his shovel into the ground—threw dirt over his shoulder. Time's a flat circle. So is the world. His conviction's contagious. 'What's the point?' Hal asks on their way back. 'The point is not knowing the point. Faith in *The Mission*.' 'Stop talking in circles.' Rick's quiet for a beat, 'I'm only telling you this because I know you'll give up otherwise.' 'That's a glowing profile.' 'We're digging to the other side.' 'What?' 'You keep asking what we're digging for—oil, treasure, something. We're digging for truth.' '...' 'We're gonna find out what's on the other side of this Flat Earth.' 'How much longer are we doing this?' 'Not much longer. Things are in the pipeline.' 'What's that mean?' 'Things are looking up.'

Carter drinks soda in the tent. His dad's attending another meeting. He's been saying they'll get a new radiator, but so far that's an empty promise. Carter wishes they were back home. His dad returns incensed—livid. He doesn't talk. It's evident as soon as Carter sees his stiff silhouette opening the flap. Carter doesn't greet him. He'd fly off the handle. Carter hears about *The Dig* and thinks about his grandma—how they couldn't dig out that toothpick and had to replace the lock. 'They might go a different direction,' Carter's dad's solemn. 'That guy—*Rick*. He's stealing my gig.' 'What gig?' '*The Tour*.' 'So, you dragged us here for nothing?' 'Have faith,' his dad says

menacingly. 'I just need to make things right.' Carter raises
the can to his lips.

THE GREAT ESCAPE

At night, the cold's worse. They're still waiting on a fully functional heater. Carter's dad relishes the frigid air. He says the wind's different—uncut—like how his mom talked about drugs. He says it's straight from the source—unfiltered—it blows flat across with no obstructing land formations. Carter doesn't know if that's true. His dad wields plausibility like a weapon. He's gone all day. Carter wants to get in the car and turn on the heater, but his father would lose it. He'd complain about the battery and how Carter never listens. He'd probably send him to a corrective camp. The kids talk about *FE Betterment Centers* sometimes. One kid was interred but doesn't elaborate. He gets distant and despondent instead.

'What do you know about that guy?' Carter's dad hovers his hands over the malfunctioning heater. He hits it, unplugs it, plugs it back in. 'What guy?' '*Rick.*' 'Nothing. Why?' 'You're always listening. He's the only obstacle between us and fortune.' '...' '*The Tour* would mean we're set for life.' 'Everyone has a crush on him.' 'You haven't heard anything bad?' 'Like what?' 'Anything incriminating—scandalous.' 'He's the best one at *The Dig.*' It's quiet. There isn't a singular tension—there are competing tensions. His dad's desire to get rich and Carter's general unhappiness. together like they were about to dig into a non-existent meal, and their friction generates heat. Carter appreciates the reprieve from the cold.

'We just have to find where the wick's hidden for the powder keg he's sitting on.' '...' 'I'll be back. Don't tell anyone I left.' 'OK.' 'I need to know you understand.' '*I understand.*' 'This is how you contribute—it's time to start pulling your weight.' Even when Carter's dad is there, he's hardly there.

Carter's dad pats Carter's head before he cuts in vectors between tents. The sun's setting. If he doesn't act fast, he'll be back at square one.

Carter's dad maneuvers circuitously and loses him. But that doesn't mean anything. He knows how they operate—following and catching people red-handed is how he got his start. He was finally climbing the ladder—living The Dream—but now that's endangered. He goes to the perimeter, stares at the flat terrain, looks over his shoulder, and starts ascending the fence. He reaches and pulls himself up. His body strains. He reaches and pulls himself up. He feels unsteady. He reaches again. Time's a flat circle. So is the world. He's close to actualizing this redemption arc he's decided is preordained. He reaches again. A vice of flesh seizes him from behind. It's the guy who was trailing him. Carter's dad falls to the ground hard. He's disoriented. He's pulled to his feet by his hair. 'You made a big mistake,' the brute says.

A MEETING OF MINDS

They're in a tin structure. The brute stands at the door like a sentry. After he unloads Carter's dad, it's like the brute dematerializes. The door opens: 'What are we going to do with you?' He sees Jeff's oblong face. His suit hangs loosely on his frame like curtains on a window. 'We've done a lot for you.' 'Like I haven't helped you?' 'It's been mutually beneficial. We even let you keep your car.' '...' 'This doesn't look good.' 'I wasn't up to anything. I swear.' 'Scaling that fence isn't being up to nothing.' Usually, there are others. Everyone's cordial, respectful, and there's a palpable unity—a communion colloquially known as radical. The table's twice as big without the others there.

Carter's dad was zip-tied and corralled. They were cloistered by the sepia deluge of night. 'You're already on thin ice,' Jeff says. 'We've already made our doubts about you explicitly clear. This isn't helping.' Jeff's eyes sear into him. They're glassy and nebulous—murky. 'Can't we let bygones be bygones?' 'Bygones? You're compromising everything. We're so close and you want to derail the momentum we've built?' 'You owe me.' 'I owe you?' 'I did your dirty work for months. I *handled* defectors and dissenters. I maintained order and paved the way for this hulking motherfucker,' he jabs his thumb toward the brute standing listless as a narcoleptic.

'You did what you did because you had faith,' Jeff says. 'You can't confer that onto us. We dispel untruth and supersede it with truth. Everything else is on you.' '*Remember Bill?* You said you were forever indebted to me.' 'You have some nerve.' There aren't windows. It's cold outside but stuffy inside from the radiator. Carter's dad sweats profusely. 'How do you think it feels to be discarded and replaced by that asshole—*Rick?*' 'How many times do we have to teach you the value of sacrifice? Rick's a better face—his story's palatable. You don't participate in *The Dig.*' 'I have a medical condition.' 'Sure.' 'Psychogenic pain is a real, debilitating disorder!' the brute reactivates—all acuity returns and he's ready to restrain Carter's dad.

Jeff lights a cigarette and deliberates. 'You're a liability.' 'A liability?' 'We're officially rescinding our offer and putting Rick on tour.' '...' 'However, you're right. You've done a lot for us. From zoning permits to discounts on materials, you've been unrelenting and *creative.*' 'I'm loyal,' Carter's dad says. 'I deserve that tour.' 'You deserve nothing.' 'Rick's not perfect. I know it.' 'How do you know it?' 'Give me a day outside. I'll prove it.' 'Prove it?' 'It's why I was climbing.' 'Listen, you still have a place here. This stays between us. This is a second chance.' Carter's dad stares at the cheap carpeting, 'Is that all?' 'Unless you have anything to add.' '...' 'Go home to your son.' Carter's dad stands. Everything aches. The brute opens the door, and a burst of cold blindsides him. 'Get Rick,' Jeff says. 'Tell him that asshole's after him.'

IT APPEARS YOU'VE MADE SOME ENEMIES

'We're leaving,' Hal said after *The Dig*. But after Rick details *The Tour*—how they'll be set for life—how it's something people like them aren't often afforded—Hal reevaluates. Rick calls his story a parable; Hal thinks that's a bit much. Hal was so adamant he didn't care openly discussing defection flouts core principles everyone's expected to abide by and uphold. It's a punishable offense. He's heard about *Betterment Centers* but investigating that wouldn't be a rabbit hole—it'd be a mineshaft to the center of the earth. But who's is he kidding? Look where he ended up.

Everything feels like a bait-and-switch—from a flat earth masquerading as curved, like influencers editing photos and using filters (Hal used to joke FEs must have serious baggage to suspect even the world is catfishing them) to a hologram moon—everything's a cosmic practical joke—like how wet dreams are nature's interpretation of putting your fingers in water when you pass out. And, if everything's a joke, why take anything serious at all? Hal takes one hit of pot before passing out. Rick's used to working like that. It's how he got by back in St. Louis:

- Wake up early
- Work until evening
- Get blackout drunk
- Repeat

Time's a flat circle. So is the world. But, still, Rick's seen this look in Hal's eyes before—when he opposed selling pot until he held all that cash. Rick retrieves a voluminous tome of FE literature. He looks erudite reading, sitting cross-legged with cigarette smoke curling around him like a time-elapsed rendering of weeds suffocating abandoned lawn furniture. It's cold outside but stuffy in their tent. Someone approaches. He keeps reading. He has an image to uphold.

Disembodied voices discuss FE ideology. 'Rick, you there?' He's more an eclipse than a silhouette. 'Who's asking?' The tent flap unzips. Rick's offended he didn't ask before entering. 'Jeff wants to see you.' '*Shh*—he's sleeping?' Rick points to Hal. The brute looks at Hal, then Rick blankly. Rick feels like he's speaking in tongues. 'Jeff needs to see you.' 'How about some manners.' '*Please.*' Rick stands, stretches, goes to the cooler, 'Want a beer?' 'No.' 'You're lucky.' 'Why?' 'You really got the gift of gab.' '...' 'What's this about?' 'Someone's out to get you.' Hal's mouth is agape.

Tomorrow, they'll return to *The Dig*. Then again the day after. Time's a flat circle. So is the world. 'It's like boot camp,' Rick said as they vacated the truck. 'Just another week of bullshit, then we'll live like kings.' '...' 'Sacrifice, Hal—it's the only way things come to fruition.' Rick stares at his big, round body leading him. People approach to shake hands, 'We're blessed to have you.' 'No, no, I'm blessed to have you.' They arrive. Rick's used to one-on-one meetings. 'Thanks for coming.' The brute puts another ashtray in front of Rick, goes to the mini fridge (specially installed for Rick), and retrieves a beer for him. 'It appears you've made enemies,' Jeff smiles.

ARMS RACE

Carter's Dad and Rick engage in history's most pathetic arms race. Every morning, they go to *The Dig*. Carter's dad stares out partially unzipped flaps with vacant eyes, vigilant like when the judge put the fear in him. 'This is our redemption,' he tells Carter. 'Destiny takes the chosen and returns them intact.' Rick doesn't tell Hal what Jeff told him. Communication there is mostly a game of telephone. Rick's heard of him. He assumes he's innocuous but eventually comes around to the gravity of things, like how Magellan (supposedly) circled the world.

Carter's dad waits silently to hear if everyone else knows. But even silence is unconvincing—absence is twice as condemning as presence. But, still, they take measures. Rick and Carter's dad stockpile whatever they can. He gets rope, wiring, and hard, blunt objects from his car—he uses a duffle bag, so no one sees him trafficking munitions. Rick isn't as well equipped. He didn't anticipate being entrenched in a rivalry—embroiled in a bastardized iteration of Cold War relations. He's at a disadvantage but can't go to Jeff or Hal because:

- **If he goes to Jeff,** who knows how that'd look. Maybe it's a test—look how quickly they discarded Carter's dad. He's aware he's on thin-ice even if no one has explicitly said it.

Most importantly, if he goes to Jeff, he'll look weak. Tattling doesn't exemplify the stoic fortitude a prophet should exhibit.

- **If he goes to Hal,** who knows how he'll react. He's itching for a reason to bail. Once he's made up his mind, there's no dissuading him. He'll suspect Rick's back to his old ways. Hal used to clean up his messes all the time. Also, he doesn't need Hal flying off the handle. Nothing's less becoming than self-recalcitrance.

Carter hasn't felt more at home in months. His dad stores a gun under his pillow. 'When'd you get a gun?' 'Months ago.' 'Have you used it?' 'No,' his eyes telegraph something different. Before leaving their apartment, things took a similar turn. When things get to this point, there's a tacit understanding Carter won't interfere. It's always been this way. His mom talked about it at meetings: 'If a recipe calls for a pinch of sugar, he uses a cup of rat poisoning instead.' Carter hopes they leave soon. The kids are intolerable—constantly trying to proselytize him.

'I need a shovel,' Rick tells the short, truculent man after *The Dig.* 'You need a shovel?' 'For *The Mission*—help me help us. Jeff won't forget.' 'Fine. But bring it back—they're still pissed I lost those keys.'

Hal's acclimating. He's even reading Rick's FE literature. But, ever since their first dig, Rick's been high-strung and distracted. 'Rick,' Hal says as they head back, 'what's going on?' 'What are you talking about?' 'You've been acting weird.' 'It's nothing.' 'Rick—' '*Drop it.*' The rest of the ride's silent.

That evening, Carter's dad intercepts Hal returning from a Porta Potty, 'I have a proposition.'

A MAN OF ACTION

The star-speckled night sky is immeasurable and clean. 'Rick wouldn't do that,' Hal says. 'You think he randomly showed up for refuge because everything was going swimmingly?' 'How are you so sure?' 'People like him have populated my entire life.' 'You really think he's playing me?' 'I don't just think—I'm convinced.' 'What do you want from me?' 'What do you mean?' 'You're here for a reason.' 'I need information.' 'Information?' 'About Rick.' 'Like, snitching?' 'Helping.' 'What do you get out of it?' 'That's unimportant.' '*The Tour*?' 'It's for *The Mission*.' '*The Mission*? Rick's the most dedicated one here. Who are you to question his commitment? You actively avoid *The Dig*.' 'I have a—' 'Medical condition?' '...' 'You should get that checked out.'

He knew they had enemies. He knew that kid's dad resented them and their station. His jealousy's the talk of the camp—how mercurial and vindictive he is. Clouds slowly cover the sky like bones encased and preserved in earth like *Tupperware*. Under different circumstances, he would've rocked his shit for even suggesting he betray his brother. But that's grounds for eviction. Then all this would've been for nothing. There's no telling how that would devastate Rick. More than anything, he didn't knock his dick into the dirt because of his kid. Hal wants beer, pot, and sleep. *The Dig* wiped him out.

Carter's dad thought it'd be easy. Those motherfuckers fouling this planet who reject *FE truth* are so gullible. They believe anything. But everyone's enraptured by Rick's performative faith—smoke, mirrors, and sleight of hand. Jeff won't help—Rick's brother won't help. He's shaking like a rat dog when he returns. Carter knows it's not from the cold, 'What's wrong?' 'You do everything for people, and they spit in your fuckin' face. That's what's wrong.' '...' 'But they've got another thing coming. I'm a man of action.' 'What happened?' 'They're fucking us. They're taking everything like we won't do shit about it!' People nearby stir; Carter hates it when his dad makes a scene. 'We have to take matters into our own hands,' his dad says with quiet venom. Carter nods. Hopefully, they'll leave soon. 'We have no choice.'

Hal gets back. Rick's reading, smoking a cigarette, and drinking beer. 'What's wrong?' 'It's—well—nothing,' he remembers how Rick snapped earlier and can't help being passive-aggressive and petty. It's like their mother tongue. 'It doesn't look like nothing.' '*Drop it.*' Rick pretends he's OK not knowing. But no one's ever OK not knowing. It's like being OK not breathing. Carter's dad's outburst echoes through the encampment. They smoke a bowl, drink beer, and it pours out like they were laxatives, 'You know that guy with the kid?' 'The one we're replacing?' 'He approached me.' 'Approached you?' 'He's looking for dirt to discredit you.' '...' 'You're not surprised?' 'No.' 'You knew this entire time?' 'In a way.'

Carter's dad sits cross-legged, gripping his gun, staring at some indeterminable point in the tent with dog-like vigilance.

THE BIGGEST MOTIVATOR

Carter can't sleep. His dad sits up all night with palpable desperation bordering on penitence. Who knows how long he sat there? Time's mangled and disfigured like mice a cat toys with—like the construct of a round earth. He tucks the gun into his waistband like in the movies. It's unclear if it's from emulation or experience. Carter wonders where he's going but has mostly stopped caring. He never gets straight answers anyway. Carter thinks about *The Tour*—about his father's compatriots—he thinks about Rick—his high hopes for Hal. He's never heard a silence so deafening. He hopes this is conclusive and they can return to the real world.

The first thing Carter wants to do when they're out is see every movie he's missed. He learned about the Amish at school—how they abstain—and now that seems like a superpower. He wants to eat candy by the pound and drink soda by the liter. Carter wants to stay up late *and* sleep in— but, more importantly, he wants a bed with a mattress and pillows. He wants to eat cereal and watch cartoons. Then he wants to see another movie. Time's a flat circle. So is the world. He wants to read books with *no* reference to Flat Earth. He doesn't miss friends—he's never had many. His parents haven't exactly primed him to be a socialite. Even FE kids with whacked-out parents don't jive with him.

Carter wants to play laser tag. He wants to clamor through sepia and neon. He wants to turn corners, pull triggers, and run in circles until time expires. They used to go all the time. They had one good experience and have been chasing it. They've gone to malls and shacks in the middle of nowhere. Every time (with one exception) it's been a bust. Like how his mom talked about chasing that feeling and watching it drift out of reach until it was unattainable, slowly disintegrating on the horizon in the distance. Carter would give anything to navigate those air-conditioned rooms—he'd give anything to cut in vectors through the darkness with no discernible goal. Though that flippancy has been a point of contention with his dad since they first started seeking out laser tag venues.

Carter wants to go so far away the stench of FE affiliation is unrecognizable. He wants to get away from these freaks for good. He wants to sit atop a hill and look out across hilly terrain, feeling redelivered as the wind caresses him, sunshine raining like confetti. But, more than anything, he wants to reassemble the life they had. He'd even take watching TV while his mom nodded out on the couch (a true Hallmark moment). He wants to raise everything they ironed flat. Then he hears it: a preternatural boom. The camp reactivates—people pour out tents and shamble toward the gunshot like common sense was too heavy a load for a flat world to freight.

SHIT RUNS DOWNHILL

Approaching footsteps telegraph sinister intent. Rick's awake. Hal identifies something different in his eyes—something buried beneath glib, charismatic charm, and piety that clawed its way out like zombies in cheesy horror films. 'Someone coming?' Hal asks. 'Sounds like it.' 'Who?' 'I have my suspicions.' 'You think he'd do something drastic?' 'Who knows what people are capable of anymore?' Hal's sweating but outside's freezing. Their noisy radiator conceals their voices. 'What's he want?' Hal asks. 'Nothing good.' 'Should we confront him?' 'Are you crazy?' 'But—' The flap slowly unzips. 'Should we call for help?' Rick grabs the shovel, 'How would that look?'

Carter's dad enters. Rick slides the shovel beneath himself. Carter's dad's feral—exuding depredation—his eyes are like what Rick's only seen in unraveling, strung-out compatriots. Rick says flatly, 'My brother says you're after me.' 'Don't try to make yourself a martyr.' 'Jeff warned me, too. For good reason apparently.' 'You're fucking us out of our fortune.' 'You fucked yourself out of everything—out of life.' Carter's dad talks manically—like they're on parallel planes talking over and under each other—one flat earth suspended over another. 'I'm a man of action,' Carter's dad retrieves the gun and tugs his collar, 'It's a fucking sauna here.'

Rick looks at the gun, at Carter's dad, at the gun, then Carter's dad. Time's a flat circle. So is the world. Hal's catatonic. 'You're gonna kill us?' Rick scoffs. 'You're in enough trouble.' 'You don't know shit.' 'Jeff told me everything—how you murdered that judge and called it a crusade.' 'Shut up.' 'How he funds your drug habit.' 'I said shut up.' 'You think I took your opportunity? You didn't need my help for that.' Hal's never had a gun pointed at him but knows not to talk to the gunman this way. 'Go back where you came from. You and your wife are soul mates.'

'Don't do anything drastic,' Rick says. 'You're just a henchman with an overinflated ego.' 'Rick, that's not helping.' 'He's bluffing. He can't even help on *The Dig*.' 'He's done it before.' They bicker about Carter's dad like he's not there. Like his parents did. He remembers trying to dig out the toothpick when he snapped—like they hit a septic tank and salient bile shot out the earth. 'I'm gonna make things right,' Carter's dad takes another step.

Rick swings the shovel. It barely misses—Carter's dad reflexively pulls the trigger. Rick slumps back. Carter's dad stands in statuesque disbelief. Hal grabs and beats him with the shovel like putting an animal out of its misery. Officially, they declared it premonition—that Rick knew his fate and they were digging a suitable grave for a man of his spiritual stature. But Hal *knows*—they hit a septic line and shit shot out the earth like fool's oil. Carter's stranded. He heard shit runs downhill. But on a flat earth, it doesn't run at all. It just pools up until you drown in filth.

*spontane long colasp (shuffling at the speed of
her trailer's light)*

I.   POWDER-BLUE CLAD GOONS

'They're holding me against my will!' Esther screeches. 'You should see the way they stare! Please help!' The phone flat-lines. The man dressed in blue garments pulls it away from her head with wispy hair like cobwebs. She's tied to her bed by ligatures. Only her feet have autonomy. She kicks out at the man observing her like something irretrievably lost. 'Let me go!' His words are unintelligible but consolatory—like he's appeasing a grousing child. A fluorescent light flickers and buzzes. It reminds her of when she was a girl and disturbed a beehive.

A cross is mounted on the wall across from the bed she's splayed on like a crucifixion. 'Help!' Her voice is haggard. On her bedside table, there's a watch and a picture of her son. Her window's a perfectly framed rendering of purloined freedom—grey as cement—cloud fragments sutured together like the skin on Dr. Frankenstein's monster. Her reflection's distorted in the windowpane. She has no recollection of getting there. One day she was in her trailer. The next she materialized here. And no one listens.

She was restrained after ripping out her catheter with a pop like an uncorked bottle of champagne—after she flung her feces at those powder-blue clad goons—after she nailed one in the gut and knocked the wind out of them, relishing watching them double over to catch their breath. Their sinister intentions were telegraphed by their eyes. Now she's unable to move the upper half of her body and can barely galvanize the lower half to do much more than writhe. She wonders who else is imprisoned and ignored when they beseech these vacant-eyed cocksuckers. Whenever she's bided enough energy, she tries breaking free. She's stopped expecting it to work but still does it, like praying.

The door opens and someone carts in food. It's a woman. She has to understand. If there was anyone she could appeal to, it's her. Esther's eyes and mouth water. 'Esther,' the woman beams, 'how's it going?' Esther erupts: 'You gotta help me.' '...' 'They're holding me against my will. I think they want to, well, I don't know.' 'Calm down—shhh—it's OK.' The woman rubs her head. It's the first time someone's listened since being tied to this bed like a dog chained to a radiator.

'Help,' Esther says. 'Please.' 'You can't go home.' 'What...?' 'But we'll take good care of you.' Her eyes turn—life is siphoned out—they're serpentine—predatory like the rest of them. 'You, too...?' 'Eat this. You'll feel much better,' the woman loads a fork with food and steers it into her mouth. 'Much better, hm?' The woman says. Esther knows better than to swallow whatever's in this meal. She chews slowly and then spits the masticated food at the woman. It sprays across her face like Newman in Jurassic Park. Her eyes widen with terror. She runs out and calls for help. Esther stares at the blemished white ceiling tiles and basks in victory.

II.   SHUFFLING AT THE SPEED OF HER TRAILER HOME'S LIGHT

It could be a day later or an hour. Things go in and out of focus like a defective aperture. The powder-blue uniforms render everyone amorphous. Like they were flattened by steam rollers. They hiss, 'You shouldn't have done that, Esther.' They have a vial of liquid. She tries reading the label, but the letters turn into hieroglyphics. 'What's that?' They attach it to the hooked rig that suspends intravenously administered fluids.

'This'll help,' they say with eyes like manhole covers, 'Trust me.' Esther jerks and contorts her body. She kicks her legs. Who knows what they think she needs and why? 'Calm down.' 'Please—wait!' Esther's eyes are a tapestry of every fear of her lifetime. 'It's for your own good.' 'I need to use the toilet.' 'You have a catheter—we tied your hands for that express purpose.' 'I don't have to pee.'

They engage in the world's most pathetic Mexican standoff. 'It's, uh, number two?' Esther nods. 'You can go after.' 'I wanna go before.' 'Let me just...' they try to finish attaching the vial, but Esther produces a raw screech—she thrashes and shakes the whole bed. They stare at her like she's possessed, 'Stop screaming—OK—*fine*—just stop.' Esther abruptly quiets. They mutter to themselves while unbinding her wrists.

Her arms haven't been by her side in days. It feels less natural than them sticking out like antennae—like a crucifixion—like she's adapted to immolation. They're vigilant for any *funny business*, as Esther would say to her son. Back when he gave a shit if she were kidnapped, held prisoner, drugged, and everything else. But these days all her son cares about is Flat Earth conviction. They help her shuffle to the toilet, pushing and rattling the rack as she slowly traverses the cold linoleum flooring.

'I'm done,' Esther says after ten minutes. 'Feel better? Now we can—' when they're close, Esther brings one hand from between her legs—she's holding shit. She rubs it in their face like clowns with pies. They dry heave—gag—produce vague approximations of words. They shamble to the sink to wash their face. This is the only way to avoid certain intravenous death or whatever these sadistic fucks are planning. Esther strains to stand and walk down the hall. She tries looking inconspicuous, but the panic's unmistakable—like hormones she's releasing.

Light pours through the pane centered on the upper panel of a door at the end of the hallway. She shuffles at the speed of her trailer's light—the one with the delay. Beads of sweat trickle down her face. She grabs the door handle. Just a few more seconds and these people can't hurt her anymore. She pushes the door open. One foot crosses the threshold. Before the other can, she's apprehended from behind. They drag her kicking and screaming to her room. When she returns, she has a roommate. They clean her up with hard, unforgiving eyes, tying her legs for good measure.

III.   SPONTANE LONG COLASP

Esther sleeps for an hour or a day. People in blue garments handle her like an unpredictable animal. A few handle her with outright contempt. Tubes run through her roommate's ribs connected to a contraption filling with dirty fluid like septic water—like a reverse IV drip. Esther can't fathom the unspeakable horrors they subjected him to—what that fluid actually is and what those tubes are actually doing. They're planning something for her, too. She asks every day and only has a vague idea. They wheel her around, drawing blood and putting her in giant, mechanical tubes like in science fiction movies. They replenish her IV wordlessly.

Esther turns to her neighbor—a true watershed moment because she's never been neighborly, and that's putting it kindly. She has a rap sheet to prove it. Just producing a pronoun sounds like it's tantamount to dislodging a bullet from her gut, 'They're going to hurt me.' He has long, thinning hair that makes him look fifteen years older. His mom visits frequently. They speak an unrecognizable language. She sits at bedside for hours, even when he's unconscious. Esther communicates non-verbally. She gesticulates like she's directing traffic.

'Listen,' she points to her ear, 'before they,' she points to the door, 'come back,' she affects the demeanor of goons reentering. Esther's heard about the Pace Tracker they're implanting in her. She's convinced it's a tracking device. She's desperate. She speaks slowly and deliberately—she enunciates every letter of every word. She looks at the machine collecting liquid—the tubes sticking out of his ribcage. 'What...is...that?' she points at it, then at her own ribs.

The young man parrots the doctors, 'Sp-ahn-tane Long Coal-asp.' Esther's mouth gapes open, 'Good God.' It sounds like an experiment. Like she's always been paranoid about being subjected to at hospitals. Spontane Long Colasp. Suddenly it makes sense—why he has to blow into that apparatus until the balls in the case are pressed against the top? He's a guinea pig. 'What did they do to you?' She sputters. 'They're putting a Pace Tracker in me,' she cries, 'They're putting a tracking device in me, and no one cares.' Her roommate's instinct is to console her.

'You don't know what's happening, but you're in trouble,' she says. It's all congealing. They don't speak English. They're not complicit—they're just unaware. It's why she doesn't trust Anglo doctors. 'You have to get out,' she says, pointing at the door. It sounds like she's accosting him. He recoils when it hits a particularly painful pitch. 'They're experimenting on you. Get out now—call your mom—leave!' The air feels like nettles. His English isn't good, but he's heard plenty of get out and leave. It's the first English he had to learn. She tries to sit up like she's going to approach him. The restraints stop her, but it's unnerving. He pushes a button, and powder-blue clad goons emerge, rolling their eyes. She's wheeled to a private room until she calms down.

IV.   THE BIG DAY

Esther's eventually returned. People enter and exit in attire that borders on liturgical—clothes suited for a ritual sacrifice. They whisper about the Pace Tracker like she's not there. The young man and his mother are cordial. They speak in their language. She knows they're talking about her. But she's focused on escaping—surviving and telling the horrors she endured. 'Tomorrow's the big day,' a powder-blue-clad man says with eyes like black marbles, 'It's normal to feel nervous, but you're in good hands.'

Esther sleeps. Spirits visit her—the usual spectral culprits. No one else visits; it's rationed normalcy that sustains her through this nightmare. Her deceased husband sits on the edge of her bed with dog-like vigilance. He rubs her head. 'Forgive our son,' he says. Afterward, she's visited by The Chinese Man, an apparition she's complained about her whole life. When recounting visits, she reduces him to a heap of stereotypes. He points at the door and taps his watch.

Esther doesn't wake up—she's catapulted back into herself. Tomorrow's the big day. It's 2 A.M. Her roommate wakes up to inhuman noises and presses a button. People enter with expressions like prison guards. 'What's wrong now, Esther?' A woman asks. 'Your roommate can't sleep.' 'Drop the act. I know what you're doing to him.' '...' 'I'm leaving,' she says. 'I'm going home.' 'You don't have pants on.' 'Then put pants on me.' 'Please—' 'Put pants on me now!' She shrugs, 'OK.'

They put pants on her. Esther says, 'I'm leaving. Bye.' 'Where are you going?' 'Home.' The woman shakes her head in disbelief: 'You'll feel much better after tomorrow.' Esther screams and thrashes, 'You can't keep me prisoner.' It takes two men to hold her still. A third injects her with a syringe. 'Let me...go,' her voice tapers off, 'I'm...leaving...' Her roommate witnesses it all—how they fit plastic bags over her legs and call them pants, and how she believes it.

Esther wakes up two hours later. She stares at the cross across from her bed. They don't feed her—they didn't feed her yesterday. It feels punitive. She calls it a hunger strike. A powder-blue goon enters, 'It's time.' 'Wait—can I do one thing first?' 'What?' He talks like he was debriefed precisely about this. 'I wanna call my son.' He looks at her bedside photo. 'Hurry. We're on a tight schedule.' If he answers, he can save her.

The buttons beep in a dissonant succession of tones. No one answers. She hasn't heard from him in months. His junkie wife ruined him. The phone flat-lines. 'Stop! Please! I don't want that tracker in me!' Her shaking bed and uncouth voice sound like an exorcism. 'Goddammit,' the man says and calls to the hallway, 'She's not going down easy.' She's eventually wheeled down the hall. 'Why the hell's she talking about a tracker?' he asks. Within a week, Esther's bumming cigarettes off her roommate's mom and boasting about recovering faster than him.

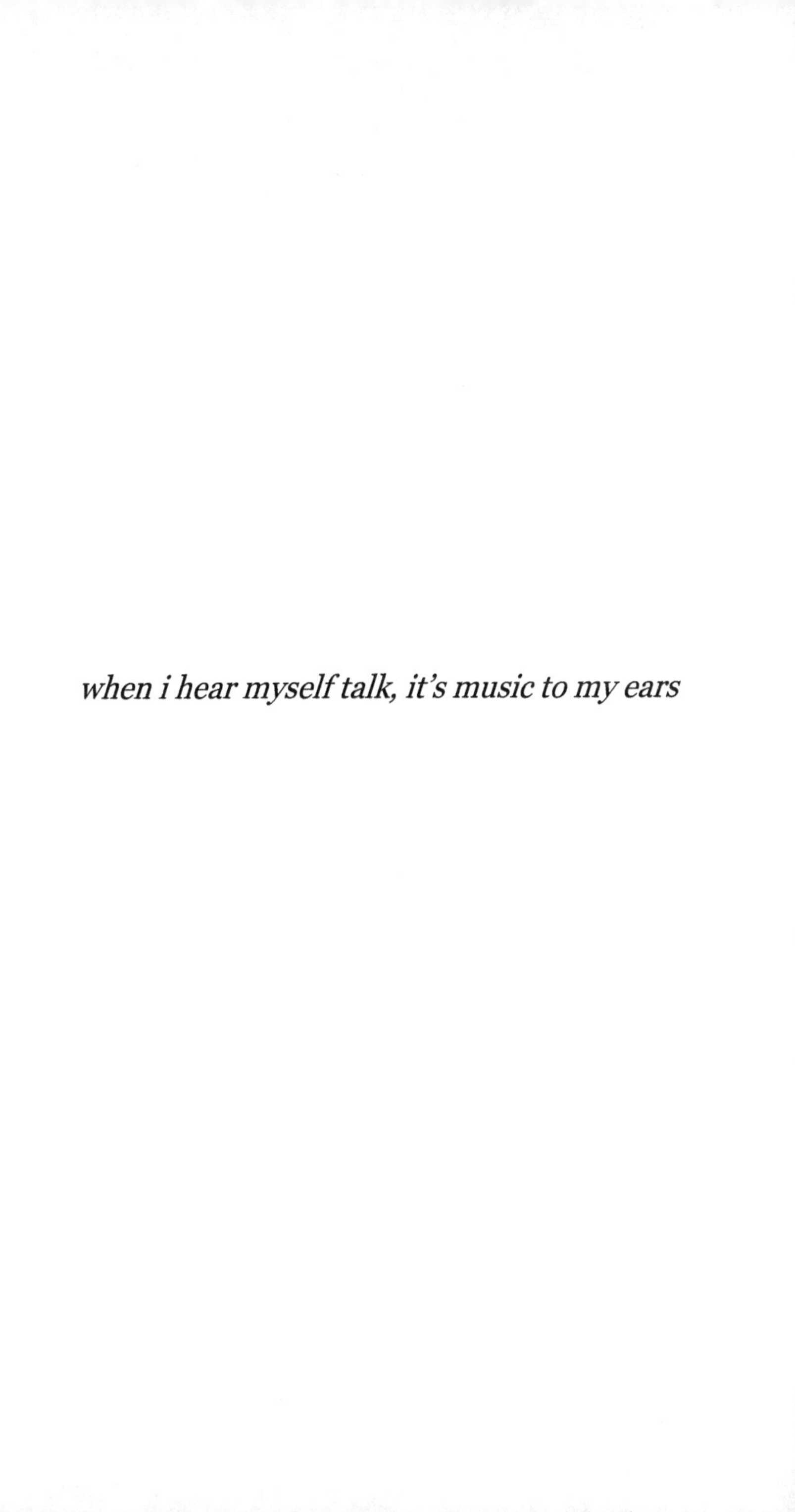

when i hear myself talk, it's music to my ears

YOU'RE NOT GOING DOWN (YOU'RE JUST GOING UNDER

Drive a while and it feels like your car's reading brail—it rattles as you traverse imperfect asphalt, uneven and divot-addled. Locals denigrate it as unbecoming wrinkles on perfectly flat terrain—like military personnel prioritizing starching their collars over maintaining peace. Signs are erected before especially rough stretches: *Warning—Shaky Road Ahead—You're Not Going Down—You're Just Going Under.* But, eventually, things smoothen briefly. Your car stops seizing with an epileptic's fervor. Equilibrium's restored. Looking around, you'll see a solitary segment of manicured asphalt. Black as the universe—level as the besieging Illinois terrain.

'Jesus,' people say after being hedged in by Illinois state lines their entire lives, 'it's like we paved over outer space.' They stare into the asphalt like an abyss, prostrated, noses brushing it while they pet it. They take pictures beside a sign affixed to an unused pole of unknown origins jutting out like a giant weed that reads: *This Stretch of Highway is Proudly Owned by Jeb Christenson.* They ask what's wrong with the surrounding run-down expanses speckled with concave, amoeba-shaped depressions—they exalt all Jeb does for his stretch of highway. Rumor is he named it Carmella, after his late wife.

While Jeb's celebrity blossomed, Jeb was unaware. A cluster-fuck of a cop in the best way, he found modest success starting a Loss Prevention agency. By business-relevant metrics, he got by all right. It even partially sated what he hoped police work would. Still, he felt unfulfilled. You can only watch so many women traffic cheap jewelry and lipstick in bras before you start asking that supremely unanswerable *why?* The only time he approached fulfillment was after apprehending a shoplifter who'd been personally responsible for thousands in lost revenue. As he pursued them, yelling, 'LP! Stop!' and as they darted through clothes racks, pushing some over to obstruct his path, he'd feel a spiritual sigh of relief.

Regardless, the legend of Jeb outstripped Jeb himself. Unmarried, his conscience was like a spouse. When it suggested he tend to Carmella, he obliged. Like clockwork, he'd procure supplies, drive 45 minutes, and get to work. As soon as he spotted an area that looked compromised—that wasn't even an issue yet—he'd touch up the section like putting out fires before they've combusted. On one such night, a driver sees someone crouched in the middle of the road.

Delirious from working the night shift, the driver squints at a man's contour rendered diminutive and spectral by the dark and distance, 'He'll get himself killed.' However, he soon realizes he's not some vagrant. He's doting on the highway like his kin. 'I'll be damned,' he takes photos, 'Excuse me, sir—' he begins. 'Ain't a bathroom for miles,' Jeb interjects, 'but you can piss on the side of the road. And *no*—I won't watch.' 'You Jeb?' 'Who's asking?' 'Your work isn't going unnoticed.' Before Jeb can respond, the truck's gone. Soon after, Jeb buys a Porta-Potty and sets it up roadside.

For the people.

DISPOSITION

A storm rattles their tin home. 'You believe this guy?' Barry asks. 'What guy?' 'This fuckin' guy?' He points at the TV. A man in a suit is holding a microphone beside a highway. Scrolling text introduces Jeb Christenson, who stands awkwardly. He doesn't know where to look—at the camera, the cameraman, the reporter, or the ground. He cycles between them until Claire feels dizzy, 'Where do I know him from?' 'How does *he* get on TV? Shouldn't it be, like, the best and brightest?' 'That's the military.' 'Still,' Barry waves dismissively, 'it oughtta be reserved for the especially esteemed.' 'Local news is reserved for anyone with time to kill.'

'I'm just saying,' Barry says, walking away, 'you should pay your dues before exuding that self-important vibe.' 'Are we watching the same programming?' 'No one should have that reach with no finesse or intent.' Barry worries about a tornado. The rain and wind whip their trailer's flanging. He wonders what they'll do in Woodcreek. Whole families relocated there. Outside is an opaque, washed-out world— all individuating traits sanded off by unrelenting rainfall and lacerating winds.

Barry checks his messages—*nothing.* Anxiety congeals in his throat like a wadded-up towel stuffed down a drain. But this isn't unusual. That motherfucker doesn't have access to phones or the Internet for most of the week—

sometimes two weeks. Every time something like this is in progress, he feels the same pangs of fear. Sometimes he wonders why he's so hung up on conning everyone but himself. If he could just mine himself the way he does others, it'd be a real *teach-a-horse-to-fish* scenario. He gets a beer and returns.

'That's where I know him from!' Claire says. 'He's gone viral.' 'For what?' '*Carmella Road.*' Claire hands him her phone, and he scrolls through the pictures of Jeb on all fours tending to the road with a toothbrush in the dead of night. 'Is this guy trolling or is he just old?' 'You earn that disposition—the distinction's never been clear.' They sit a while longer. Jeb talks about his highway—he gets choked up looking at it. He wipes a stray tear from his cheek with the back of his hand and apologizes, explaining it's hard to keep your composure intact when you're proud.

'You got kids?' He asks the anchorman. 'Two.' 'Then you know the feeling.' 'Um, sure.' Barry doesn't hear from that asshole all night—the longer it takes, the more he hopes a tornado catapults him across the flat terrain like a shot put. Barry rolls a joint. Jeb announces he's installing toll booths. He's tired of negligent highway adopters corrupting his section, but he takes no pleasure in doing it. When asked if it's amenable, Jeb responds, 'One thing I've learned working LP is there are certain faculties in certain people that can't be rehabilitated. They can only be demolished and rebuilt.' Barry lights the joint, exhales, and says, 'That motherfucker's off his rocker,' like he's impressed.

BAD BLOOD

Jeb hears it on the radio a week after his news appearance. He's stopped going home. It's less a decision and more a natural progression. There are several reasons:

(i) Firstly, there's nobody to go home to. It never bothered him until Carmela. Now, his empty house is an index of abject isolation.

(ii) Secondly, he worries what people might do—whether it's disgruntled residents spiting him or envious highway adopters spiting her.

(iii) Lastly, and similar to the last, he can't go home. His fall from grace was a precipitous plunge into an abyss. Threats have proven substantial.

Jeb's in a tollbooth, staring across the flat immeasurable Illinois terrain, Carmella safe beneath him. After his news appearance where he exuded the confidence of a fat kid wearing his t-shirt into the pool, things took a turn. He had no idea he was revered until he was universally despised. People refuse to use Carmella on principle. It's hard to not think he's talking about *them*. 'All he cares about is money,' people say. 'That fame went to his head.' 'I'll be damned if I pay him to use that road.' 'He's as bad as FEs.'

But Jeb's only aware of the most salient views and pervasive opinions. It's the nuances that hurt. Unsurprisingly, he's not big on Internet usage, which insulates him from the vitriol. 'Money,' he scoffs. He's motivated by something far more significant—something that eclipses money. It's not his fault other highway adopters can't get their shit together and nobody recognizes what he's doing. He's even considering selling his business to redouble his efforts on Carmella. Eventually, the only cars that approach are driving into town and quickly make a u-turn because they:

A) have heard about this lunatic playing sentry

   or

B) aren't willing to pay a toll on principle.

As long as they aren't traversing and desecrating this sacrosanct stretch of road, Jeb's done his part. He only returns to town at three a.m. for supplies. At that hour, he only gets occasional sidelong glances and can operate, more or less, unperturbed. Half the stores still owe him one for catching thieves. They help but make sure no one finds out.

Jeb hears it on the radio a week after his descent from folk hero to conman. There are two roads into town. One's been stymied by Jeb's tollbooths. The other's so congested with cars—so saturated with people spiting Jeb—people sit in traffic for days. Some die in traffic and it's not discovered until road rage spurs someone to action, which transmutes into heartbreak. He's like God the way he's moved the masses.

He resolves to prove a point, too. A vehicle eventually approaches from town carrying a woman in labor. 'I know there's bad blood,' the man says, 'but it's an emergency. How much? I heard it's a few bucks.' 'That was before.' 'What's it now?' '$1,000.' 'You're joking.' 'One thing everyone seems to get wrong about me: I'm not the jokin' type.'

DO NOT DISTURB

The TV's muted when Barry gets the text: '2night. Same time.' Barry doesn't respond. He's always waiting and can only tolerate so much before making a point. Though that asshole probably won't realize this is remonstration. The trouble with retribution is you can't afford to be subtle— nuance gets in the way. 'You need the truck tonight?' Barry asks Claire. 'I have a business ethics class.' 'I need it.' 'What do you mean you need it?' 'I it.' 'When?' 'Eight.' 'Drop me off, then. My class starts at seven.'

This is the culmination of two weeks of stress. The stereo's static with a spattering of generic pop music. Claire bobs her leg when it's possible to discern rhythm. Streetlights streak by in coruscating swaths. They arrive and Claire says, 'I'll wait here. My class finishes at nine-thirty. Don't take too long—I have work tomorrow.' 'You and me both.' '*Work*. You could use a business ethics class.'

Barry's distracted. As far as he's aware, she told him to have a good night. He drives to the church FEs convene in. They have their compound, but it's still the epicenter of recruitment. Barry smokes a cigarette in the car before entering. It'll be less suspicious. He surveys the parking lot and approaches clandestinely. The spare key's under a mat. Even sanctity has lost all sanctity. He goes to the meeting room, sips dregs of stale coffee, and has a cigarette.

He hears the door open and hopes it's not a priest. Though they afford these FE crazies a peculiar license. Like degenerate relatives they're obliged to tolerate and can't help commiserate with. He hears the clipped gait and in enters a distended, pale emaciated man with a splay of disheveled hair. A prophet's constitution. 'Glad you could make it, Barry.' 'Wouldn't miss it for the world, Rick.' 'So, the re-up.' 'You're not wasting time. No pleasantries?' 'Pleasantries are a luxury—we have people to subdue.'

'I can sell the same volume.' 'We discussed a discount.' 'The best I can do is 5%.' 'Rich said I could count on you.' 'Rich says a lot of things.' 'You're not the only supplier.' 'Good luck finding another while that lunatic blockades us with tollbooths.' 'He's all right—that's the kind of conviction we could use.' 'What kind of conviction?' 'Simple conviction.' '...' 'Fuck. Fine. But Jeff's gonna expect something to give next time.' 'Maybe all we're looking for is commitment first.' 'We'll see.' 'I'll deliver tomorrow.' 'I'll leave the money in the same spot.'

Barry asks, 'What do you mean you've got people to subdue? This shit works like that?' 'The only thing comparable is faith.' Barry's quiet and Rick leaves. Barry refills his coffee, has another cookie, and smokes one more cigarette. He contemplates the money he'll make. They'll finally have a guest trailer. He's so busy daydreaming he forgets to pick up Claire. He goes home, gets crossfaded, and thinks about how all ladders look like the Eiffel Tower on their side before passing out.

ADJOURNED

A meeting's in session. Barry hoped it was AA, NA, or anything else. A man speaks at the podium like he's delivering a sermon. Lights hum above enraptured people raising botched coffee to their lips. The speaker says, 'You can stare across a Flat Earth right into your destiny. It'll all make sense.' 'What will?' A bearded man asks. 'Everything.' The package is in a book bag. He was expecting to grab the money behind a ceiling tile, supplant it with the package, and leave.

He suspects Rick arranged everything, so he'd meander into a meeting—an elaborate ruse to proselytize Barry and get a discount on good faith. Because Barry can't drop off drugs without being noticed. Even if he was intrepid, these aren't people you want to have access to your shit. He's sold to half the assholes in attendance. Barry stands in the doorway, sees people smoking, and lights a cigarette. A cork board's behind the speaker with pinned-on pictures of nondescript, flat terrain indistinguishable from each other and identical to the Illinois land besieging them.

The speaker notices him, 'You gonna stand there all day?' 'I was just passing by...' 'That's what they all say.' 'Who?' 'Latent FEs.' 'Latent?' 'I know what you are.' 'What's that?' 'One of us.' Barry wants to say he's a drug dealer and not an FE because that feels more dignified. 'Take a seat. We don't bite.' Everyone's eyes sear into him, and he finds a seat. The room smells like God's unwashed asshole. People take turns speaking in circles—detailing how FE conviction changed their lives. They say for the better, but it's unilaterally for the worse.

'I was fired,' one says. 'I lived in my car. All for FE belief. It's persecution. But now I live at *The Settlement*—I have my own tent.' From an apartment to a tent—a real riches to rags story. It's like they're not talking about FE ideology at all—like it's a surrogate. He thinks about that highway-obsessed motherfucker. How he couldn't tell if he was trolling or just old. Like when he first met Rick caked in dirt. 'I was digging,' he explained. 'For what?' 'We're not digging for something. We're digging to something. To the other side.' 'You really need more drugs?' Rick just laughed. But look at Jeb now—the world's putty in his hands.

Still, this craziness is preferable to the tumult at home. After forgetting to pick up Claire, what ensued was trench warfare. A brutal war of attrition where neither side gained ground. He was half-drunk when he woke up and volleyed his own barbs. He's dreading talking about it. Accountability's overrated. After all, look where he is. After another hour of tangential, double-speak that's more subtext than substance, the meeting adjourns. People file out; Barry sits. 'You staying?' The speaker asks. 'I need a minute.' 'That's normal for first-timers.' Barry waits then takes the cash, leaves the drugs, and studies the cork board one last time.

PASSAGE

The cold used to feel like an Indian burn. Now Jeb barely notices it. Refusing a pregnant woman was an inflection point. The sky's all fragments—warped clouds like shifting tectonics—a funhouse mirror reflecting the earth. Sometimes light filters through. Most times it doesn't—most times it's an index of desolation. Time doesn't move; it congeals. Jeb looks at Carmella, allegedly named after a late wife—as if he's ever been married. The closest he came was when he was 28. A girlfriend was going to enlist, and they planned to marry. She cheated and he promptly ended things.

For the record, her name was Bethany. After that, he found himself embroiled in a series of doomed relationships, but nothing notable or substantial. His subsequent partners weren't named Carmella either. The name's from his favorite show, *The Sopranos*. His infatuation with Tony's wife developed into an unhealthy attachment. Jeb stopped going to town. He stockpiled goods a week ago. They won't last long. He's starving himself out to starve them out. Last night, someone called to schedule a meeting about a partnership. He stares down the road at the town like swallowing a gun's barrel.

They said *they endure unending persecution themselves*, and *that should engender solidarity*. Jeb sits beside an ineffectual radiator. Birds streak across the sky.

They look like fish cutting in vectors beneath ice. Jeb's happy with whatever assistance he can get. His employees call supplicant for help—they're floundering. Jeb says he can't leave—says this is bigger than LP, him, and them. He doesn't know what exactly, but he feels the magnitude. He feels it in his viscera—his guts.

Jeb stares across the steely, even terrain and sees a truck approaching. There's solace in this flat terrain. He doesn't know if it's the guy who called or someone else— someone seeking passage or with sinister intent. He grips his gun, though he hopes he doesn't have to discharge it. He's never had to, let alone at another person. The truck stops a mile out and someone exits. Hair a greasy entanglement, patchy beard—pale, tall, emaciated. With hands in the air, he shouts, 'Jeb? It's me—Rick. We spoke on the phone? Can we talk?' 'Yeah.' Each step is incremental magnification.

'You've made quite a name for yourself,' Rick says. 'It hasn't done much good.' 'You'd be surprised by how many you inspire.' '...' 'Like us—at *The Settlement.*' 'The compound?' 'We avoid that word—it has connotations.' 'I used to think FEs were off their damn rockers. But lately? Shit, I don't know.' 'Jeb, we know what you're going through. We know people are on your ass and we know you're vulnerable out here, especially alone.' 'I can take care of myself.' 'For now. Things eventually come to a head. We can help each other. You control this road, and we have *resources.*' 'What do you want?' 'Nothing, really—passage for designated cars.' 'What are they to you?' 'Don't worry about that.'

87

for designated cars.' 'What are they to you?' 'Don't worry about that.'

I'M NOT OUTTA MY MIND (YOU'RE JUST OUTTA YOUR ELEMENT)

Rick calls over a week later. The reception's so bad it's a cacophony of interposing voices—disembodied—a spectral whirlwind—a landslide of lapses and static. Barry doesn't know where they get the money. Before Rick, his income was subsistence level. Soon, he'll never have to work again. It's the American Dream. Though Claire would say he's not exactly working now either. He says he's doing it for them like a mantra. That she'll never have to intern herself in another classroom again. With his leverage over Rick, he can set the price to anything.

Barry waits in his car a few minutes before going inside. There's nothing more suspicious than someone like Barry idling in an empty church parking lot at night. Gouging Rick feels like a service fee for how often he waits for him. But Barry tolerates this to sustain their business relationship. Because where else is he gonna get a client with an unregulated, built-in addict's retreat? Plus, who knows whom else he's selling to? Interims between re-ups have shrunk and Rick seems entrepreneurial.

'This shit's selling like hotcakes, huh?' Barry asks. 'It sells itself.' 'You want the same amount?' 'First, let's talk business.' 'Isn't this business?' 'We want a discount.' 'It's not in the cards right now. I'm sure you can understand.' 'Well, you see, I can't.' 'Then you're gonna have to learn to.'

'The chickens eventually come home to roost.' 'By the time they return, I'll have enough money to put them out on their ass.' 'Maybe you won't.' 'What do you mean?' 'Remember that lunatic with tollbooths?' 'Yeah.' 'I visited him. We struck up an arrangement.' '...' 'I learned you have to create your own opportunities—that's the genesis of *The Settlement*, after all.'

'What are you getting at?' 'Your competition will give me the discount I want if I get them passage to procure product. That lunatic and I hit it off. I told him I'd keep his tollbooths secure if he admitted designated vehicles.' 'You're outta your mind.' 'I'm not outta my mind—*you're just outta your element.*' 'What are you asking for?' 'Well, I tried negotiating all nice-like, but that was a bust.' '...' 'What was I asking for? 15%? Let's make it 25%, and I want you to move munitions for us. Sound like a deal?' 'For you.' 'We can always open the levee and see where things fall.' '...' 'Sleep on it.'

Rick doesn't shake his hand or say goodbye. Barry's left standing in that same room he saw an audience eating up FE bullshit in. He wonders if they're better off—if surrender is key. Because everyone's doing it. He smokes a cigarette, stares at that loosened tile they've been using for exchanges and thinks about a lot of things. Mostly, he thinks about how he hopes Claire hasn't dropped her class already and how he could end up back here. Except not as a businessman. As something hardly there at all—acclimated to the times.

WHEN I HEAR MYSELF TALK, IT'S MUSIC TO MY EARS

Jeb sleeps in the tollbooth. One of the guards left for burgers. The lines are unconscionable. They stopped getting their shipment of frozen beef and had to resort to fresh-slaughtered beef. While the quality vastly improved, it took a while for people to acclimate. The other security guard is in the opposite tollbooth. 'These men are at your disposal,' Rick said. 'We're committed to you.' He's hulking, reticent, and always looks asleep even when he's not. Jeb wonders if this is an elaborate ruse and he sold out.

He wakes up sporadically. Sometimes it's the blustering wind; sometimes it's the cold. Tonight, it's footsteps. Probably Security Guard 1 returning. He doesn't know their names. Asking was a dead end, but maybe asking Security Guard 2 was where he fucked up. The footsteps are light and subdued—muted. Jeb walks out, hoping he didn't forget ketchup. He'd even take pickles. He looks up, and he's face-to-face with a rifle-wielding, plain-clothes vigilante.

'You Jeb? You match the description.' 'What's the description?' 'I'm here to hurt you—not your feelings.' '...' 'You're hurting people, and you don't care.' 'You can't understand. This is something greater.' They rub their temple, 'Shit, don't tell me you're an FE, too.' 'I'm not—but they're friendlier you assholes.' 'I heard you were chummy with them. Even when you were worried about corrupting your highway, I knew. The ones worried about corruption are always the most corrupt.' 'I'm the one being ousted and persecuted.' Jeb's eyes dart to Security Guard 2.

'Make a peep and I'll blow your head off,' he says, 'Things don't have to escalate.' 'What do you propose?' 'We want things the way they were.' 'The way things were wasn't any good.' '...' 'What do you do for a living?' 'I'm in between jobs. Why's that matter?' 'It just explains why you're not a master negotiator.' '...' 'I'm not tearing 'em down. As long as I got Carmella, I'm fine.' 'Do you hear yourself?' 'When I hear myself talk, it's music to my ears.' 'You need help.' 'Considering the circumstances,' Jeb looks at the rifle, 'I'd agree.' 'You fucked us.' 'You fucked yourselves. I'd love nothing more than to decease on Carmella.'

'You crazy motherfu—' A shot rings out and they collapse with a dry slap. Security Guard 1 is standing with a smoking pistol aimed where the rifleman was standing, and therefore now at Jeb. His other hand holds a brown sack; a soda's nestled in the crook of his arm. 'You mind lowering that thing? It's aimed right at me.' 'You've made enemies.' 'Who hasn't?' 'I haven't.' Jeb takes the brown sack. There's a burger with NO PICK scrawled in charcoal black lettering. 'You're an angel. I have to admit,' Jeb says, 'I'm coming around to this whole dispatched sentry deal. I'm starting to think me, you, and Carmella is one big happy family.' Security Guard 1 stares at him blankly before returning to his car. Jeb gorges himself in the tollbooth.

WAITING LIKE HE'S AT THE DMV

Jeb gets a call explaining there's been an incident. Rick was shot in his tent. The voice lilts with emotion that feels like mustard gas. They're inconsolable, which works out because Jeb's not the consoling type. They say, 'I'm calling because things are changing.' 'Changing?' 'We have to recentralize. Regroup.' 'Do you guys ever say what you mean?' 'There are a lot of moving pieces, Jeb.' 'The world is moving pieces—it's all moving tectonics.' 'I see why Rick liked you.' 'I only met him a few times.'

'Can I talk to John?' 'Who's John?' 'The guard.' 'I don't know their names.' 'What have you been calling them?' 'Security Guard 1 and Security Guard 2.' 'Can I make a wild assumption?' 'Shoot.' 'John is Security Guard 1.' 'Why?' 'Lenny's barely there even when he is.' 'Big fella?' 'Mm-hm.' Jeb exits the tollbooth, shouting, 'John!' Security Guard 1 approaches like he never expected Jeb to say his name. He takes the phone, steps away, and speaks in an incomprehensible murmur.

He's never heard that harrowed intonation outside of films and one occasion he caught someone stealing merchandise to pay their mom's medical bills. Someone from *The Settlement* came, loaded the rifleman in the bed of a pickup truck, and redelivered him to town, dumping him in the center to send a message. He thinks about them lying dead on Carmella's incomparable, smooth surface. He wonders if Rick lay in ignoble, crooked, distorted death, too—stiff and lifeless—dignity siphoned out—juxtaposed against perfection. But mostly he wonders how to get the bloodstain out of Carmella, and how these motherfuckers ruin everything even in death. John hangs up, 'We're leaving.' 'Leaving? Someone just tried to kill me—you just killed someone to send a message.'

'We just follow orders,' John shrugs. 'Will different people be dispatched?' 'Probably not.' 'What about the cars I'm letting through?' 'All Rick's schemes are *donezo.* You're welcome to join us.' 'I'd rather die out here.' 'Suit yourself.' John gets Lenny. They get in the truck without saying goodbye and disappear into the distance. Jeb doesn't know what to do—*he has blood on his hands.* He wonders if he should've gone with them—but that would've meant leaving Carmella. And a life without Carmella is no life at all. 'We'll figure it out,' Jeb pets the asphalt.

Unsure what to do, Jeb tries to get the blood out. He clips weeds, picks up trash, and goes into Lenny's booth. It's the finishing touch on Carmella's renewal—on eliding all evidence those motherfuckers were ever there. He feels used—conned—*dumb.* He finds Lenny's lighter and cigarettes. It's as good as finding money. He retrieves one, steps out onto Carmella, and stares at the town, taking a deep drag, and exhaling, he says, 'This is how it was always supposed to end,' to no one in particular, not even Carmella. The town soon discovers what happened and galvanizes—mobilizes. Jeb's waiting when they do like he's at the DMV.

LIFE ISN'T SUSTAINABLE

Even with Rick's discount, Barry's earning in a different stratosphere than he was—in what's more like fragmentary recollections of a past life than one he remembers living. Between the booze, pot, and other extracurriculars, he's adopted a standard of living he refuses to forfeit. Barry's 6'2 with a frame you could mount a TV on but never thinks about it unless he sees someone taller. Because if they're tall to him, they must be tall. Only guys mention it. Like a compulsion. Never rude; more astonished. Like, 'You're a big guy. You ever play football?'

Barry can't tell if they're implying he's fat, which always bothers him. He never played football but sometimes says he did. Claire's stopped going to class. Partially because she was looking for an excuse. But mostly because Barry insisted. She couldn't use their truck because he was always using it. But she's seen the money he's making with that creepy cult affiliate. They're watching the news when Barry's phone rings. He's online shopping. Delivery trucks are fixtures. Even Claire admits she could get used to it.

Barry's drinking beer and parceling product. His body goes taut. 'You good?' Claire asks. 'Yeah.' 'You think it's about the discount?' 'Dunno.' 'You think he wants a bigger discount?' 'Fuckin' hope not.' 'Maybe he'll offer to pay full price if we can, like, do something for him. Maybe that guy's a bargaining chip.' 'Maybe.' 'You gonna answer it?' Barry answers, 'Hello?' 'Barry?' 'Who's this?' 'Rick's colleagues.' 'Wackjob compatriots, huh?' 'Rick mentioned you were a pleasure to talk to.' 'What's up?' 'Rick was involved in an altercation.' 'What happened?'

'He's dead.' 'Dead?' 'He was shot and killed in a tent.' 'Jesus.' 'We're all broken up about it.' 'It's anti-climactic, no?' 'Trust us, Barry: You're preaching to the choir.' 'You have a choir now? What do you guys sing, hymns about a world sanded down?' 'Listen, Rick was industrious—always facilitating moving pieces. Now there's no facilitator. Our priority is regrouping—recentralizing.' '...' 'We're terminating our arrangement.' 'I just got the package he wanted. That's outta pocket.' 'We're sorry, but this was unforeseen. To a degree.' 'To a degree?' 'Let's just say he made some enemies. Good luck, Barry.' They hang up abruptly.

Barry puts his head in his hands, 'Fuck.' 'What?' Claire asks, 'You said this was a sure thing.' 'Rick's dead.' 'Dead?' 'It's some real biblical shit.' 'What's that mean?' 'They're terminating all his business arrangements.' 'Like, all arrangements.' 'Yeah.' 'Including ours?' 'Yes.' There's a beat of silence before Claire says, 'Maybe it's for the best. How long was this gonna last? It's unsustainable.' 'Life's unsustainable.' 'You can start building a career. You haven't exactly been on the ball lately.' 'What do you call making this kind of money? Off the ball?' 'You haven't worn real pants in months.' 'The only people who wear real pants are people who haven't figured out how to make life work for them.' Claire rolls her eyes and Barry gets another beer.

97

THEY THINK THEY HIT ROCK BOTTOM

They don't descend for days. It instills a false sense of security. Maybe Rick was a master tactician. Maybe it wasn't some con. Most importantly, maybe this shit isn't a zero-sum game. '*Maybe, baby, I'll have youuu...*' Jeb hums. Across the terrain, Jeb sees someone approaching. He reevaluates his skepticism: maybe there's salvation in a Flat Earth. Jeb spends his days pacing Carmella—looking at her reduces him to tears. At night, he stares at the star-spangled sky and scoffs at how even infinite doesn't compare.

Initially, Barry considers Rick's sudden departure, as FEs say, a minor setback. Rick proved to be a man of his word: he admitted cars carrying enough weight to reset the market. Barry's habits outstrip his means. He stays up all night, feverishly drinking, smoking pot, and railing lines. Claire tells him to slow down—rein it in. He assures her it's under control. One night, it hits him like an epiphany. Rick's gone but the clientele isn't—all that's disappeared is his liaison.

Jeb clutches his pistol. Watching the plain-clothes vigilante drop dead affected him more than he'd admit. The truth crystalized that he was never supposed to be a cop. He's been fated for Carmella his whole life. This is immolation—sacrosanct. He's no martyr to anyone but the two of them, and there's no one else in this cock-sucking world he'd want to be a martyr for. A man and woman emerge. 'Jeb,' he says, '*enough's enough.*' 'We're helping you,' she says, 'Things are gonna get messy. A man's dead, Jeb.' 'I'm no stranger to messes,' Jeb says.

Barry leverages transactions into learning everywhere FEs convene. Those apprehensive about divulging sensitive information are persuaded by discounts and complimentary product. Barry attends meetings, speaking with born-again conviction and fervor. Afterward, he sets up shop like selling Girl Scout Cookies. Initially, he talks with an affect but wonders if he's manifesting belief—speaking it into existence. Like how he started saying *bro* ironically and accidentally integrated it into his lexicon. Each meeting moves him toward the two-dimensional. 'I stare across the flat terrain and sometimes forget to be grateful,' he omits this because he can see people coming miles away. Still, the more he says it, the less that matters.

Jeb's statuesque. Within hours, cars approach. He has one last cigarette and pets Carmella. He murmurs sweet nothings—says it's only goodbye for now. They'll spend eternity together—the afterlife—clean, measureless, flat—everything that makes Carmella perfect. Then he stands straight, aims, and starts firing. They return fire. Within minutes, Jeb's splayed across Carmella, bleeding out, thinking this is the only dignified death he could've died. FEs catch on and oust Barry. That FE shit sustained him and now he's unmoored and rudderless. Without FEs, he's relegated to his former strata—barely scraping by with worse habits. Claire reconsiders school while Barry atrophies on the couch. They think they've hit rock bottom until they sell their trailer for parts.

backpedaling forward (the great neighbor erasure)

Days move so fast the sun hurdles us. Transfixed by reversion, we stare at the lurid sky—the great annihilator — shattered—shards rejoined, creating interstitial space for oblivion to percolate. Our eyes are mirrors you could do coke off of. We stare skyward in puritanical supplication— jaws gaping on defective hinges. We have three cigarettes left, so we split one. I hold the smoke in my lungs like pot before passing it to Carter, who does the same before passing it to Jess, who returns it to me. Like a relay race. Time is a flat circle. So is the world. We haven't felt the wind in months—months spent undulating between insubstantial sleep and sweat-drenched stupors—feverish and delirious. Stumbling upon stretches of time serendipitously and formulating schemes to transcend it all. Rebuffed by fate—rejection, eternal and ubiquitous. Rejection is what God was supposed to be. Lately, it's so hot

my skin hurts. We are what we've tried our damnedest not to be—alive. We sip malt liquor from 7/11 coffee cups. Try pretending otherwise. Going through the motions like playing house when you're little. Like when I played house in pre-school with Sarah, whose interpretation of the game was putting a doll up her shirt and yelling at me about getting a job.

We'd smoke pot, but we forgot the pipe. More embarrassingly, our pitifully aggrieved contingent can't roll joints. Let alone blunts. Third-rate survivalists in a world coming apart. We have a tent. In case we have to live off the land. Repopulate the planet. Carter, Jess, and I. A polygamous future for a limp-dick world. The food chain is wretched gravity—shackling us to a plunging ship. Anchoring us. Fattening us up to keep us in place. Self-sustenance is a pipe dream. An uncooperative zipper can mystify me; nothing would stultify and disarm me as much as survival. Nothing would reduce me to a catatonic heap of obsolescing organs quicker. 'What *was* that?' Carter sputters. We resent him asking. We just wanted to brush past it like a loon at a rest stop accosting drivers—continue without acknowledging what we witnessed. 'What could've screeched across the sky like that?' 'Dunno,' I say flatly, 'and I don't wanna find out.' The world scales down to my periphery—collapsible and retractable. I focus on what I can control; I focus on nothing, and it helps somehow. I don't care if Carter doesn't like my answer, and I don't care if Jess doesn't care anymore.

I take a measured sip of brew and the cigarette eventually returns—it makes a revolution—completes its orbit. Time is a flat circle. So is the world. 'Maybe it's, well, *you know*,' Carter says. 'Christ, Carter,' Jess exhales in overwrought aggravation, '*get a grip.*' Carter doesn't say anything, but he feels denigrated. He just doesn't realize it yet. It takes him a while to metabolize these things. But neither Jess nor I care at this juncture. I contemplate turning around. Retreating back to The Territory. Absconding this grotesque drive to survive. But it would be anathema to my nature—these instincts piloting me like a drunk convinced they drive better after having a few. Carter and I never really liked each other but we've been best friends since he showed up at school after living on that wacko Flat Earth compound. We're like begrudged, conjoined twins who are, ideologically at least, misaligned and incongruent despite being grafted together by God himself—diametrically opposed—like a cosmic practical joke or reality show premise. Like mismatched shoes worn because no matching pairs are available, and you can't leave the house barefoot. 'What will the *neighbors* think?' My mom (R.I.P.) would say. Even after The Great Neighbor Erasure, she'd repeat this mantra and suffer neighbor-induced neurosis. She'd manufacture them like we manufacture God(s).

'What are we gonna do?' ornate, rococo terror festoons Carter's staccato voice, 'What *can* we do?' Jess' body goes taut and tense. Her drugged eyes and facial features reconfigure like shifting tectonics, telegraphing unadulterated annoyance—facial features rearranging like the glacial clouds creeping over us and the besieging interminable, arid landscape. The air is surfeit with a surcharge of electricity—fricative and palpable—a frequency that passes through us like specters—like an imperceptible, besieging dimension of death. The world is a haunted house we're playing house in. 'We'll keep driving,' I say, 'fill up at the next gas station, and keep driving.' '*We'll* drive?' Jess scoffs. 'Last time you said that, you passed out drunk and I drove five hours straight.' 'I provided moral support.' She can't suppress a smile. Even Carter lightens up—decompresses. We hear it again; then we see it. Like a sequence of thunder and lightning. The screech and then the streaking *thing.* A coruscating, evanescent swath superimposed over the discolored, hemorrhaging sky. A sky like dried blood stains on a cream-colored shirt. A sky more like a crime scene than the threshold to paradise.

They said it was coming; we just laughed; now the joke's on us. I go back to the car and sit on the hood. Jess sits beside me. I stare at my lap. Take a sip of brew. Light the second to last cigarette ceremoniously. Hold it longer than I should, then pass it to Jess, who puts her head on my shoulder. Her hand on my hand. It feels good. Carter eventually rejoins us. In degenerate magnanimity, I offer the last cigarette. 'Have that to yourself,' I say, 'you need it more than us.' Carter smiles but that disguised insult smarts. He lights it, and we stare upward. We've lived our lives like a gas leak, slipping into stretches of unconsciousness only to wake and navigate the world with somnambulant intent. But now it's sneaking up on us like edibles we forgot we took. We stare up at the vacuum where the sky used to be. Transfixed by reversion to existence so temporal it's embarrassing.

Acknowledgments

Thanks to my mom, Beth, and dad, Michael, for always being there for me and believing in me, and to my girlfriend, Nikita, for putting up with me and supporting me unconditionally. Thanks to my brother for always supporting me even when I go AWOL. Thanks to my Uncle Paul Rodriguez for drinking with me. I'd also like to extend a special thanks to Josh Dale for believing in my work and Caterina Alvarez for being patient with me (which is definitely an understatement) and helping me bring this to life. Thanks to Joshua Silva for believing in me and for inspiring me to be creative and do good work. Thanks to Kevin Kurcz for being one of my biggest supporters. Finally, thanks to Sergey and Lenny for working on so many projects with me.

About The Author

Joshua Rodriguez is a writer living in Tijuana, Mexico with his girlfriend. His fiction has been published in *Door is A Jar Magazine, Expat Press, FIVE:2:ONE Magazine, Silent Auctions Magazine, Black Flowers Journal, Heavy Feather Review, Purple Wall Stories, Sledgehammer Lit, Loud Coffee Press, Fugitives & Futurists,* and *Maudlin House.* He also authored the novella, *FAMINE: Get the Hell Outta Here While You Still Can* (Alien Buddha Press). Find him on Instagram: @yungtrompoking

About the Publisher

Follow us on:

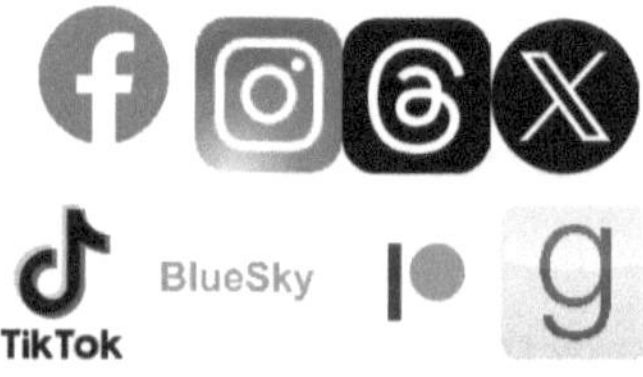

Scan the QR code to visit

www.thirtywestph.com

www.ingramcontent.com/pod-product-compliance
Lightning Source LLC
Chambersburg PA
CBHW061549310726
48972CB00008B/2671